Colours

Patty Guthrie

Ark House Press
arkhousepress.com

Cataloguing in Publication Data:
Title: Colours
ISBN: 978-0-6457514-4-4 (pbk)
Subjects: Fiction

Design by initiateagency.com

Dedication

To B.B.
You make me a better Christian.

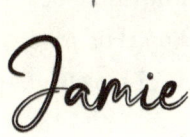

1

Jamie

His hair was longer than it should have been. It clung to his shoulders, resting in soft, hazelnut curls against the nape of his neck and bouncing as he nodded his head to whatever music he was listening to. Studying the nods and shakes, each song was wildly different from the next. One moment, there would be a slow roll from left to right, like there was a lilting symphony, pulling his mind this way and that; the next, he looked like a puppy trying to chase a bee, keeping up with the rapid ups and downs of a drum beat.

Luke wished he knew every song on Jamie's playlist off by heart.

It was their last year of high school, and while everyone was caught up in the stress of finishing school, in had walked Jamie Smith, with his winsome smile and sun-streaked hair.

He had moved from Bulli on the south coast with his Dad at the beginning of the year. Luke had heard that they had wanted a fresh start in the eastern suburbs of Sydney, after Jamie's mum had passed away at the end of last year. They had met on the first day of term, when their Modern History teacher had put them together to help each other get started on their assignment for the term, to find someone from the past hundred years who had changed history. Even though he had received the notification at the end of the year before, Luke hadn't thought about it at all over the holidays, so at least they were starting on the same page.

He forced himself to look up at the board and realised there were only a few minutes left of the lesson. His page was blank, an apt representation of his mind. He just hadn't been able to focus since Jamie had started at school.

The first problem was, the guy smelled incredible. Sitting next to him was like being at the beach; even at the end of the day, the guy smelled like he had just stepped out of the ocean. And over time, Luke had come to realise that he was also funny and clever, and history had gone from something he had to just get through to something he looked forward to, like one of Pavlov's dogs salivating every time they heard the bell ring. Until he realised that he wanted to be more than just Jamie's friend - he had a crush.

The last second ticked over and the bell went. Luke scooped his bag up, blinders on, and headed for the door. It was the middle of summer and all the windows were closed, trying to make the slow swirl of the ancient ceiling fans meaningful somehow, but he could still feel sweat crawling down his back, leaving a tell-tale trail on his white school shirt. He needed to get out.

"Luke!" It was Mikayla. Part of him wanted to hang back to let her catch up, but he could still see Jamie in his periphery and he couldn't shake his thoughts. Thoughts of asking him out, asking what his favourite movie was, living his teenage rom-com dreams. It had been taking a little longer every time.

He ploughed ahead, swarms of students seeming to leap out of the walls just to get in his way.

"Luke!" She was more insistent this time; they had known each other for so long that she had almost trained him to hear her. And obey.

"Watch it, dickhead," someone growled as he shouldered them out of his way. The hallways were tiny, and they felt like they were shrinking every second he was inside.

"Sorry," he whispered, eyeing the doors to the quad.

"Lucas Rivers, I swear on the King of the Bees that if you keep ignoring me, I am going to crash tackle you to the ground."

Luke stepped out into the sunlight and inhaled until he could feel the humid air killing the butterflies in his stomach. The King of the Bees were Mikayla's favourite band, but despite all her love for them, he doubted he would even feel it if all fifty-three kilos of her did land on him. He turned to see Jamie behind him step outside the hall and walk a few metres off to the side, sitting cross legged on the floor by himself, earphones still in. Luke turned to face Mikayla, sinking onto the concrete and swinging his backpack around so he could get out his lunch.

His best friend was short, blonde and be-freckled, with a smile which could light up a whole room and a voice which could be heard from across one when she was trying to whisper. They had met in primary school, when the teacher had seated everyone in alphabetical order to try and help them learn how to spell their names. Mikayla Norma Macnamara had started kindergarten already able to spell her name, and a hundred other long words, and brought her purple, sparkly pencil case, almost bursting at the seams with every piece of stationary she could have possibly needed for her first day of kindy. Luke's mum had forgotten to pack a pencil.

At that point, his mum had just had his little sister, who was taking centre stage (foreshadowing who she would be as a person for the rest of her life) and he had been lucky to walk out of the house even wearing a school uniform.

They had stuck together ever since, Mikayla helping Jamie out with everything from homework to life advice and him, in return, listening to whatever topic she was most interested in at the time.

"Did you see him?" Concerningly, for the last two years or so, it had been boys.

"Jamie was sketching again today. He looked like an angel, with the sunlight behind him and everything." She sighed comically and set her bento box on the floor - Mikayla's parents were very keen on the whole multicultural thing. Even though they lived in Bondi, they had sent her to a public school on purpose, to really 'get a feel for it all'. Luke pulled out his vegemite sandwich.

"He should have been focusing, I guess. Miss said that was all the stuff we needed for the maths exam." Luke hadn't heard a word of it either. "Jamie's so smart, he probably doesn't need to listen. He probably knows all of it already, like, instinctually." Luke studied his best friend as she stared at her sashimi, not really seeing it. He wondered if he looked that goofy when he thought about Jamie. He hoped not.

***

That afternoon, as Luke and Mikayla walked home, Jamie was all she could talk about. It had been that way for at least a week - the two of them had art together alone, so she felt the need to recount every moment he may have missed in their budding (imaginary) relationship. He counted the street signs they passed, and gave her a gentle punch on the arm every time a yellow car passed them.

"Spotto," he would say, and she would go on talking as if she were walking by herself.

"I wonder who he's taking to the school formal?" Year 12 had started at the tail end of the previous year, so people had been talking about the formal for months. "I mean, by this point, most of the girls have picked the guy they wanted to take, so surely he's too new to the school to be anyone's choice?" Every once in a while, he looked up at his friend, focused on the concrete like a bloodhound, trying to figure out how she was going to get closer to this boy. He wished he could admit he had been wondering the same thing.

For years, it had felt like his best friend knew everything about him, sometimes even without him having to tell her, but now, walking beside her, he was sure she didn't know how much he wanted to talk about Jamie too. How much he wanted to tell her all of the things she had missed in Modern, tell her that he also felt sick to the stomach in the best way every time Jamie walked by. He wasn't sure why - she wasn't even a Christian, and would probably be fine with it - but he wasn't ready to share it yet, with anyone.

"Wait, I thought the guys were meant to ask the girls?" he asked, kicking along a pebble with the side of his school shoe.

"Oh Luke. So sweet, so naive." She chuckled and continued musing on the sort of colour which might suit Jamie's suit and tie while matching the dress she had planned to wear since she saw it in Frankie magazine two years ago. She still had the picture tacked up on her bedroom wall. As they rounded the corner and saw the spire of the church, she asked suddenly, "What about you?"

Luke looked up at his friend and ran the question over in his mind. What colour would he pick to match his tie with Jamie's, without being the same one? Did guys even do that sort of thing, and who would buy the corsage? "I don't really know what I'm doing for the formal, at the moment. No one's asked me." With a start, he realised their school formal was only six months away, and he hadn't thought about it at all. He didn't even know whether he wanted to go.

"Well, if things don't work out with Jamie in time, you can always share a limo with me." Seeming satisfied with her own solution, Mikayla started off down her street, waving behind her. He had always thought they were going to share a limo.

"I always enjoy our little chats," he called after her. "Bye, Mickey!"

"Don't call me Mickey!" she yelled over her shoulder with a smile.

He walked through the front gate, pushing it closed behind him. Maybe the three of them could go together?

His dad was kicking a soccer ball against the wall of their house, bouncing it back towards himself. Luke slotted himself in between easily, throwing his bag down on the grass. Their dachshund, Brick, was watching dutifully from the sidelines, waiting for the ball to put a hair out of place. He was old enough to know not to sink his fangs into the ball, after many scoldings as a puppy. He had decided that simply seeing it to its destination was enough, and maybe chewing on a consolation tennis ball if the urge got too strong.

"How was school today?" Peter Rivers asked, disturbing his train of thought. He asked this question every day, almost habitually. He was a tall, lanky sort of man, who had to readjust the microphone on the lectern every time he had to speak. This had led to a permanently arched back, as if the man himself was a question mark. He operated on questions, his declarations seeming to turn upwards at the end, inviting you to answer back. Perhaps this came part and parcel with being a minister – so much of your job was chatting to people and getting them to try and open up. Luke knew it was his duty to reply the same way every day, not to break the rhythm, like the ball going back and forth.

"It was alright." Both men kept their eyes on the ball, not making eye contact but still feeling the presence of the other nearby, the soft thud, thud of the ball keeping time.

He had thought about mixing things up a million times, saying what his sister Ellie must be saying to his mum right now. 'Today at school, I saw a boy with his shirt off. He looked at me from across roll call. I think he likes me. Can you give me any advice on how to ask him out?' But, as with many unspoken rules, Luke could feel an invisible line there, not to be crossed.

"Learn anything interesting?" his dad asked, not missing a beat.

"Nup," Luke replied, and kicked the ball back.

"What are my taxpayer dollars doing at your school then?" His dad laughed at his own joke, despite the fact he had made the same one so many times before, and they continued their back and forth in silence, the church next to the house casting them in shadow as the sun began to set.

For his whole life, Luke had grown up learning about God, the Bible, church life, and a billion other little things he probably didn't even realise were a part of him, as though he had been sitting in a vat of ink and was only now starting to realise how much of him was stained. Although he had never really heard anyone talk about being gay, he had heard snippets here and there. Confusing, mismatched and usually negative snippets. He got the feeling that any discussions about having a crush on a boy would be uncomfortable at least and disastrous at worst. So, for the past few days, he had only sat next to Jamie in Modern, when they were expected to work together. He avoided him in the hallways and had stopped saying hello. Every lesson he felt like he was just holding his breath, and trying to distract himself in class had also meant distracting himself from work, so only a few weeks into the term, he realised he was falling behind. They barely knew each other, and he wanted it to stay that way - every time he got to know Jamie a little more, he could feel his crush grow.

He looked up at his dad as mum called them in for dinner. Their afternoon scene had finished and now it was time for the dinner script, with added roles for mum and his sister.

Luke wondered if the script would ever change.

2

Friends

Every year their school participated in a program which required them to learn a skill, improve their physical fitness, volunteer and go on a team adventure. As captain of the football team, Luke had already fulfilled his fitness commitment and had gone on the hike with Mikayla and the rest of the group at the tail end of the last year. Although he wasn't sure what skill he was going to learn, there was a group of students who had been considering visiting the local nursing home as their act of volunteering. It beat helping out at homework club after school - after all, he needed all the help he could get with homework himself. So that Wednesday, after school, the two of them set off to the local old folk's home.

Mikayla had seen in a documentary that almost half of the people in nursing homes don't get visitors at all, and when they walked inside, it was easy to see why.

The hallways were freezing cold, an immediate shift from the balmy weather of the afternoon outside. Everything was a stark, clinical white, with bland art lining the walls depicting country landscapes or greyish, inoffensive animals like koalas and cats. It was as if all the colour had been sapped from the world around them. Both of them could hear their footsteps echoing as they walked, an accompanying teacher's voice the only other sound as she told them to be quiet and not to disturb any of the inhabitants. As they walked down the corridors, they saw bodies lying in beds, staring out windows. Then there was the smell - a particularly old person smell, like stale sweat, medication, menthol rub and perfumes bought from the chemist.

As the students crowded into the visiting room, the teacher turned to face them.

"You need to be respectful of these people, Year 12," she said. "Many of them have lived three or four of your lifetimes and they have stories to tell. Some of them just want to be heard, and you can do them a great service just by listening to them, trying to ask questions and get to know them. There is a lot you can learn yourselves."

The group turned and looked at those seated in the room, elderly people sinking into overstuffed arm chairs, some next to untouched plates of blanched vegetables and grey steaks, others staring aimlessly at chess boards. Some were lying so still, Luke had the sinking feeling they were dead and no one would realise until the end of the day. He pictured himself, in his late seventies, eighties, nineties, sitting in one of those chairs and shivered.

Nurses walked over and gave everyone a name tag to stick to their shirt, as each of them was assigned an old person to talk to. Luke watched as Mikayla went to sit next to a woman with more of a beard than he could currently grow, and started to panic. She flicked him a grimace as she walked towards her fate. Maybe this had been a mistake. A stern looking matron called him over to a small elderly man sitting with his legs crossed at the knee in a beige armchair near the window.

Although he must have been at least sixty years his senior, Luke immediately liked him. The man was wearing shiny patent leather shoes, a cream collared shirt with an emerald green bow tie, and a navy tweed jacket. He looked as if he were ready to stand up and go somewhere, unlike some of the inhabitants of the nursing home who looked as though they hadn't been anywhere in quite some time. Next to him sat a half empty cup of tea and some mystery novels, along with a weathered old Bible. It had once been gilded with gold but now only retained the faintest glimmer after many years of pawing through its pages.

"Well, good afternoon," the old man said quietly, as if his breath had just been formed into words by a clever manoeuvre of his mouth. "My name is Elmer Richards, but some people around here call me Fuddy." He reached out an old, gnarled hand for Luke to shake, and he noticed that all of the fingers were slightly bent, as if curled around some invisible bar.

"Why do they call you that, sir?" Luke asked, grasping the hand as gently as he could. It felt like a strong breeze could snap Elmer like a twig.

"Oh, for a multitude of reasons," the old man smiled, leaning forwards. "Maybe because I go a bit red in the face when I get passionate about something; maybe because, believe it or not, when I was your age I had red hair just like yours. The cartoon, if you know him, was known for his big red moustache and his legendary chase after a 'wascally wabbit', although I can't say I've ever caught one myself." Luke was familiar with the old cartoon, it was one of his dad's favourites. "I suppose a young man like yourself may think at times during our encounters that I'm an old fuddy duddy too." They both laughed.

"Well, it's nice to meet you, Mr Richards, sir." The old man waved away the formalities. "My name is Luke."

"Ah Luke," Fuddy leaned back in his chair, intertwining his fingers together as he found some thought in the archive of his memory. "A doctor and a scholar, was Luke. A Greek name, if I'm not wrong, meaning 'to give light'. Is your father in some religious trade, might I ask?"

"Yeah, my dad is a minister," Luke smiled, surprised.

"Of course, with a name like Luke. Well, I am pleased to meet you. I hope your time here won't be too wearisome. I know you're here to get up your volunteering hours, but if you need to learn a skill - I could always teach you the art of winning chess, or how to get yourself out of a tricky conversational faux pas?" He raised an eyebrow cheekily.

"I already know how to play chess," Luke said.

"Oh, my boy, not how to *play* chess, but how to *win*." The old man chuckled.

As the old man taught the younger various techniques at a game he thought he had been pretty good at, Luke found himself losing track of time as he enjoyed himself. Despite the age gap, they had some thoughts and ideas in common. Luke had never been an avid reader, but Elmer, it seemed, had read almost any book he mentioned. If he had never heard of it, Elmer would encourage Luke to describe the story so they could still chat about it, giving his perspective on even the silliest of novels he had read as a kid.

The rest of the afternoon flew by as the two men talked and heard about each other's lives, equally interested in the foreign worlds they had grown up in. Elmer had grown up going to a boarding school and eventually gotten a job as a secretary to a famous author, spending hours transcribing his dictation on an ancient typewriter with stiff keys, hence the fingers. At some point, he had tried writing himself, only to find that he had given his best years to a stranger with not so much as a credit on a back page.

For the first time in a long time, Luke felt heard. Here was someone who didn't have to rush off or was waiting for him to finish so they could jump in with their own story. Living far away from his father's parents, and his grandparents on his mother's side having passed away, he realised he missed having that sort of person to talk to in his life who would just want to listen.

When the time came for the students to leave, they shook hands once more, promising that if they were both there at the same time again, they would find each other and continue their conversation. Afterwards, he met up with Mikayla to walk home together, eager to debrief.

"I had absolutely the *worst* time," Mikayla jumped in.

Her little old lady had whined all the time about the new generation - the one which didn't respect their elders, or stand up for the elderly on the bus, or value their country enough. The one which Mikayla was a part of. "She smelled funny and she was so *mad* about the world. It's like no one had ever done anything kind for her, like even her kids had put her in the home and forgotten about her." She waved her hands about animatedly as she spoke. "I stand up for people on the bus!" He realised he hadn't even asked Elmer how he had ended up in the home. Did he have his own children who had forgotten about him?

"What about you?"

He could feel the blush creeping up his face and felt almost guilty admitting that he had enjoyed himself. He kept the details scarce, worried that Mikayla would want to swap and he wouldn't have a good reason not to.

***

The week passed without much else happening.

Luke continued to avoid Jamie during classes, and continued having to listen to Mikayla talk about him as he if were the best thing since sliced bread. He had started to notice that she never asked him if he had his eye on anyone, but didn't want to think too much about why that was. He hoped it was because she assumed he would tell her if he did, not that she hadn't thought to ask.

At the end of the week, as the two headed home together, Luke got ready for one of the other common scripts in his life.

"Youth is on tonight - you know you're welcome to hang around if you want," he asked as they reached the gate to his house.

"I've got a lot of homework to do, sorry," Mikayla said with an exaggerated wince as she continued along the path towards her house.

They had been having that conversation almost word for word since they were kids. Mikayla's family weren't religious, but she had always taken it a step further, as if she couldn't understand why anyone else would be.

"See you on Monday then, friendo," he said, shoving the gate open with his shoulder.

Every Friday during the school term, kids from the area would hang out at their church.

There were games, a short talk and discussion groups afterwards, but most kids were there for the snacks or to mingle with the opposite gender. Recently, Luke had been interested in neither, but the church hall was right next to his house. To add to that, since the beginning of the year they had always been rostering him on for something, so it felt like he was letting people down if he didn't go.

Despite the heat of the evening, he pulled on a black hoodie and headed over.

The hall was wide and empty, with floor to ceiling glass windows on one side, letting the afternoon sun in. There were cracks and dents in the walls from rough and tumble games and bunting was strung from the beams. On one wall was a mural, depicting some biblical scene or another, faded with age. Luke had spent almost his whole life running around this hall and every corner was filled with memories from growing up. This afternoon, other than a group of girls giggling off to the side, the hall was almost empty.

Other than Jamie.

He was standing by himself near the snack table, scrolling through his phone. His long, curly hair hid his face. The group technically had a 'no phone' policy, but either someone had been lenient on the guy because it was his first night, or nobody had even noticed him yet. The leaders sounded like they were still having a meeting in the back room. Luke walked over, pretending to make a beeline for a packet of chips.

"Hey, it's Jamie, right?" he said, trying to look nonchalant.

The other boy looked up, his curls framing his face. "Oh, hey!" A radiant grin cracked across his face. "Yeah, Jamie. Luke, from history?"

"Yep!" He leaned on the table next to Jamie and immediately stood back up as it wobbled precariously. *He knows my name*, Luke noted. He swallowed the lump in his throat. "How did you end up here?" He tried not to sound too curious.

"My dad saw the sign out the front and thought it might be a good way to meet kids in the area." Jamie slipped his phone into his pocket and turned to face Luke. "It isn't exactly easy to make friends at school when you're only starting in Year 12."

"Well, I'm glad you know me but there aren't that many Year 12s who still come." Since their final year had started last term, people his age had started dropping off like flies. He probably wouldn't see them until they were invited back for the Christmas party.

"Do you come every week?" Jamie asked.

"Yeah, usually, but I guess it's kind of expected." Luke started to fold his chip packet in half, trying to get it as small as possible. "My dad is the minister of the church." There were a few younger kids starting to straggle through the front door, a youth leader appearing with a tablet there to welcome them in.

"Oh, that must be… cool?" Luke shrugged.

"It's alright, I guess." Out of all the words he associated with being the pastor's kid, 'cool' was rarely one of them.

"But do you come because you like coming or because you *have to* come?"

Luke thought it over and realised that he didn't have an answer. He had been going since the first week of Year 7, and had gone to the kids club before that. He figured the church was expecting him to become a leader once he graduated as well.

"I don't mind it," he said eventually. "I mean, it's a bit of fun on a Friday night, and a good chance to bring people to hear about Jesus." When was the last time he had brought along a friend?

"Or learn new stuff yourself," Jamie added. Luke bit the inside of his lip - when was the last time he had learned something new?

In primary school his parents had paid for him to go to keyboard lessons.

A young woman had turned up in a demountable near the playground, and every few terms the teacher would change over. A twenty-something would turn up with a bunch of worksheets, always overwhelmed with figuring out the job, and start with the basics to make sure everyone was on the same page. However, that meant every time there was a new teacher, Luke had started again from the beginning or been put up the back by himself. Towards the end of Year 6, he started offering to help out. Recently, youth had started feeling like that - he came without expectations, and was sometimes just a helping hand.

"Do you know much about the Bible? I mean, did you go to church back in Bulli?"

"Not really," replied Jamie. "I mean, my dad and I didn't, before my mum died. It's more something she was into."

"Well, you can stick with me tonight," Luke said, giving Jamie a playful punch on the arm. "I'll take care of you."

The other boy grinned and, seeing one of the younger boys do it, went over to chuck his phone in the box.

For the rest of the night, the two boys stayed side by side. They were in the same discussion group because of the year they were in, and Luke tried to let Jamie know all of the things which might be a habit to a regular, like where the toilets were and that they had to sign in every week. Jamie didn't share any prayer points or offer to pray for someone else, but Luke realised that was probably weird for someone who hadn't grown up going to church. If ever it got too quiet, a leader would always volunteer him to add something in. Usually he would try to be vulnerable, if only to encourage the other boys in the group, but tonight, with Jamie there, he just mumbled something about upcoming assessments.

By the end of the night, he felt like he knew the guy a little better, which was both good and bad.

On the one hand, Jamie, it turned out, was really funny and seemed to be brave enough to answer some of the easier, opinion based questions even if he didn't know the Bible very well. It seemed like he had been listening during the talk, which was something even Luke struggled to do most nights. He felt more comfortable being himself here than he had at school, and found himself enjoying youth for the first time in a long time.

On the other hand, what had started out as a tiny crush was starting to grow into deeper feelings the more he got to know him. It was hard to ignore how nice it felt to be the centre of his attention, and he felt those butterflies smashing around in his stomach even just sitting together. It was clear that just avoiding him wasn't going to be enough, especially if he was going to keep coming back on Friday nights.

After youth, his dad came over to greet the parents and found Jamie's dad, looking as helpless and lost as his son had. The boys jogged over to join them before anything particularly embarrassing was said.

"Jonothan!" Luke's dad reached out to shake hands.

"Please, my mates call me Jonno." The other man broke into a smile and for a few moments, looked exactly like his son. "Nice to see you again, Peter."

Jamie looked like a carbon copy of his father from the past. There were stories worn into his face - a scar above his eyebrow, greying hairs, worry lines which might only be a few months old. Jonno's skin was a deep golden brown as well, as though he had been left in the oven for a few more minutes than his son, and there were freckles up and down his arms. He looked kind, Luke thought. They both did.

"It's so good to see you again," his father was saying. "How are you both fitting into Maroubra?"

"Yeah, it's been a bit tricky getting our bearings, but I think we're on our way, hey?" He looked to his son, who nodded.

"Well, if you and Jamie are free some time, we should have you over for dinner. Were you thinking of coming on Sunday?" Luke's dad asked. "That is, if tonight didn't scare you off, Jamie?" The two boys grinned at each other, and Luke felt the wonderfully awful mix of feelings returning to his stomach.

"Yeah, I did want to check the place out for myself," Jonno nodded.

"Then come by our place afterwards," Peter Rivers smiled and Luke was impressed, as he had been before, at his dad's ability to make people feel welcome within minutes.

"Sounds like a plan."

Once everyone had left, Luke's dad sighed as they headed back to the rectory together.

"They've got a very sad story, that family."

"Really?" The two ambled slowly through the church yard, both thinking about the Smiths.

"His wife was a very strong lady, a believer, and contracted cancer. They went through the ups and downs of it for years, the church praying over her and seeing different doctors all over the place until finally, last year, she was able to rest in peace. He was a wreck, he told me. Everything around the house and their area reminded them of her, so they moved."

"How do you know that?" Luke asked, thinking of his friend. Why hadn't he thought to ask?

"I met the dad during the week for a coffee after he emailed the office asking after any programs we run for youth. Apparently the both of them continuing to go to church was a promise they made her when she was sick. It's very good of him to honour that promise. He said they weren't really church goers before this."

Luke headed inside and poured a glass of water, draining it in one go.

"People are funny that way," his dad said, pausing at the foot of the stairs. "Some people would cite suffering as the reason they *can't* be Christians, and then you've got people like the Smiths who have let it bring them *closer* to God."

He poured another glass of water and went to sit on the couch next to Brick. His faithful dog thumped his tail a few times before going back to sleep. He stroked his long, floppy ears, soothed by the soft velvet as he ran them over and gently between his fingers. Occasionally he would agitate the sensitive hairs and his dog would stir or sleepily drag a paw down his face to ward off anything disturbing him. He paused for a moment to think about the week and all that had happened.

He didn't often feel lonely, but there were moments every once in a while where he wished for a friend. Someone to fill the gaps in conversation between him and Mikayla, someone who he could just talk to as a guy. It had always been hard to talk to guys his age, worried that maybe he'd fall for them or, even if he didn't, that he would want to come out one day, and they would still reject him.

So, he hadn't shared his feelings with anyone, not even Mikayla, although they had started liking boys around the same time. He wasn't even sure whether she realised that he didn't - couldn't - like *her,* although they rarely ever talked about their crushes to each other. But now here was Jamie.

Brick grunted in his sleep and pushed his head until it was nuzzled in Luke's palm - more pats. He smiled and ran a thumb gently down the groove of the dog's forehead, rubbing the fur on his cheeks as he leaned in, his paws twitching.

When the thoughts came, he tried to let them drift on by, like pieces of litter in a river. But it couldn't be that way forever. One day, the build-up would have to be dealt with before it started to cause trouble.

3

Dinner

The service on Sunday night was almost empty. Their church had been going through the book of Leviticus, which was a tough gig as it was, but they usually only had a crowd of thirty or so young people to begin with at the night services. Tonight, they had started with fifteen.

He saw Jamie as soon as he walked in, watching from the stage as the band finished practising. They smiled at each other, but Jamie and his father had both gone to sit in a pew further up the back. His usual spot was second row from the front, right on the edge so that he could get up to play piano in the band, but it was typical for their little church to fill up from the back to the front rather than the other way around.

People were still trickling in as the service started and an elderly lady named Rose opened up in prayer. As she did, Luke found himself caught on the words, 'your kingdom come, your will be done'. He had been thinking about tonight since Friday, when his dad had invited the Smiths over for dinner and felt trapped between looking forward to it and dreading it. Everything seemed to be a mix of good and bad these days and he was just waiting for something to finally be definitive. He figured that in all of the mess, he should also be wondering what God's will for the situation was.

What was God's plan for him in all this?

For the whole night, he found himself trying to inconspicuously turn around to face Jamie when he could, or missing beats during the songs, when he could look at him while pretending to concentrate on the lyrics on the screen behind his head. He missed the entire instrumental of a song, jumping instead straight to the verse and having to repeat it so that the singers and other musicians could catch up. Jamie tried to mouth along with the words, even though it looked like he had never heard the songs before.

The sermon that night had a lot to do with blood and ancient religious rituals and Luke found himself tuning out. Even though it was past six, the last rays of the summer sun were still making their way through the stained glass and casting colourful reflections on the walls and pews of the old church. People had been gathering here to worship for over a hundred years, and yet it still felt so removed from anything his dad was saying from the front. Maybe the whole Bible felt removed from the real world, his world, right now.

He pushed the thought away.

Within an hour, the last song was played, the last prayer was prayed, and the two families were sitting down around the dinner table.

"Wow, that was a great sermon tonight, Peter," Jonno began by saying, pulling a bottle of wine out of a long brown paper bag. Luke was the only one who seemed to notice his mother raise an eyebrow as she finished setting platters of food on the table. "I had no idea about any of that history stuff, to do with the tabernacle and sacrifices. Pretty gory stuff sometimes though, hey?" Again, Luke was struck by how much he knew just from growing up around church and how much he took for granted. He started to regret not paying much attention to what his dad had said.

"Yes, certainly. It gives a lot of context to the death of Jesus, doesn't it?" Luke's father pulled three wine glasses from the back of the cupboard to add to their water glasses. He almost couldn't recall the last time he had seen his parents drink more than a light beer, but Jonno was already unscrewing the cap of the bottle and pouring for his mum.

"Just say when, Mary," he said, the burgundy liquid sloshing against the sides of the glass.

"When!" his mum cried out almost immediately and a little too loud. If Jonno noticed, he didn't let it show as he started pouring for his dad.

"When," Peter Rivers said, a little quieter and little later.

"Would you mind saying grace for us, Luke?" his mother asked, looking over at him expectantly. He could feel everyone's eyes on him, waiting for him to do something he did almost every night and yet was temporarily forgetting the words for.

"Dear Lord," he began, and saw Jamie's dad exaggerate putting his hands together, reminding Jamie, who was staring around the table, confused as to why everyone had suddenly seemed to fall asleep. "Thank you for this food, for the hands that made it and the people around the table to share it. Please bless it to our bodies. Amen."

The Rivers repeated 'amen' in unison as the Smiths went to reach for the food.

Freaking heck, Luke thought, *we must sound like a cult.*

After the opening speed bumps, the night went by smoothly.

His sister, Ellie, had seated herself across from Jamie so that she could stare at him unabashedly and ask a million questions without being interrupted. His friend looked as though he had been caught in the headlights of a semi-trailer. There was no stopping Ellie once she got on a roll.

Luke was suddenly hyper aware of all of the things he had never really noticed before, like how faded the tablecloth was and that most of the plates had chips around the edges. Jonno Smith continued to ask his dad questions about the sermon as the two of them shared most of the wine and his mother sipped and nodded, occasionally encouraging one of the teens to eat more. Ellie was wearing more makeup than usual, and she was doing this weird fluttering thing with her lashes like there was something in her eye – with horror, Luke realised his sister was trying to flirt.

For dessert, the Smiths had brought ice cream cones and, despite the fact that the four Rivers were lactose intolerant, they took one each and politely said thank you.

The parents had been talking about everything from theology to what it had been like back in Bulli and Jamie's father, Jonno, seemed to be enjoying himself. Every time he mentioned Jamie's mum, it looked like his brain buffered for a few seconds, caught between the story he was telling and what it made him feel.

"What did you think of the service?" Luke's dad asked at one point.

"Oh, everyone was really lovely and we liked the songs, although a few of them felt a bit… dated." Luke had been saying the same thing for years about playing hymns at the evening service. "They sounded like the songs you always hear sung in movies, or in that episode of Mr Bean where he kept falling asleep. Not to say I was!" he added hastily. "As for the sermon, I think I got it, but it did feel like I was going in a bit blind."

"Yes, sometimes it is easy to forget that not everyone has the same level of church literacy. We call it 'Christianese'." Both men laughed. "Did you have any questions?"

Jamie's dad looked uncomfortable, but at some encouraging nods from Luke's parents, started to form words around what had confused him. "I just don't get…" Jonno had turned serious all of a sudden. "I don't get why he would do that. God, I mean."

"Do what?"

"You know, I think at the end you were saying that after all those years of sacrifice, Jesus was a sacrifice. I've certainly got enough experience trying to pay off debts, so the idea of owing someone for your actions makes sense, and bringing the animals to the tabernacle. But then, after all those years of doing it that way, Jesus dies instead. I just don't get why he would do that."

At this point, the whole table went quiet. Jamie and Luke were both looking at Peter Rivers, who looked as though he were taking his time to handle something precious properly.

"Well, the problem with making a sacrifice every time you do something wrong is that you will always mess up again, right? Which means lots of sacrifices, but it also means that the problem isn't really solved. All this blood is spilled, but people are still sinning, they're still far from God. So, God sends a hero. One last sacrifice which would mean there aren't any sacrifices anymore."

"Once for all," Jamie said, echoing the words of one of the songs they had sung that night.

"Exactly," Peter replied.

"But that still doesn't answer *why* he would do such a thing," Jonno insisted.

"Why would anyone give up their life to save others?" Peter asked.

"Glory," Luke answered.

"Love," Jamie said at the same time. Everyone turned to look at him – even he looked surprised that the word had come out of his mouth. Turning red, he continued anyway. "When mum was dying, she went through a bunch of different tests so that doctors could try and figure out what was wrong with her. She gave blood and stuff, and was really disappointed when she found out she couldn't donate her organs or anything, but she knew that it might help save other people in the future."

"I think you're both right," Peter said, as Jonno reached an arm around his son and gave him a squeeze on the shoulder. "John 3:16 says that God so loved the world he gave his only son, but there are plenty of passages in the Bible which says that knowing we are saved will naturally lead to glorifying God and *wanting* to. I'm sure the people who your mum helped would be so honoured to know that she would do that for them."

Although he had been hearing the same thing for years, and even saying the same thing to other people, the thought struck Luke as if for the first time.

Glory and love, a mixture of both.

He knew he was loved by God, in his head.

So why didn't it feel like it?

At the end of the night, as the evening began to wind up and even Ellie had headed off to bed, Luke and Jamie sat out on the front lawn, waiting for the adults to finish talking.

"Man, what a night," Jamie said, sitting on the grass and crossing his legs to greet the little dachshund as it came bounding across the grass. "Who's this?"

"Brick." The sausage dog turned at his name and his excitement was renewed at discovering he had *two* friends to play with. "You know, because he's kind of long, and red," he grunted as the dog jumped to put his little paws on Luke's chest. "And weighs a tonne." The boys laughed as they play-wrestled with the dog, caught between the two of them. Luke reached over to grab a tennis ball from the bucket under the barbeque. "I hope tonight wasn't too intense or anything," Luke said, rolling it across the grass for Brick to go and find in the dark.

"What do you mean?" Jamie asked, listening to the fence groan as he leaned his back against it.

"You know, coming to church and then dinner with my family. Oh, and then having to deal with Ellie."

"Yeah," Jamie made a face. "I don't mean to alarm you, but I'm pretty sure she's in love with me." Both boys laughed as Brick trotted back, proudly bearing the ball. He dropped it by Jamie's side hopefully, nudging it towards his open palm. "Actually, I was kind of relieved."

"Why?" Even just by the glow of the porch light, Luke thought he saw Jamie blush.

"To be honest, I thought you didn't really like me." It was Luke's turn to go red. "It's just that," Jamie hastily clarified, "the first few days I was at school, you sat next to me in almost every class we had together. Then, all of a sudden, it was like you couldn't stand to be around me, like I'd done something wrong. I mean, you talked to me on Friday, and that was awesome, but I didn't have the guts to ask if I'd offended you."

"Oh man, I definitely didn't mean to give you that impression," Luke said. *I just didn't want to give you the opposite impression,* he thought.

It had never been about distancing himself but protecting himself. As long as his crush didn't go any further, he didn't have to think about the consequences, where it would go or what it would mean. He hadn't stopped to think about how that must have felt for Jamie, how lonely it must have been as the new kid to have the one person who you were actually starting to get along with suddenly not even want to be near you.

But how were they supposed to be friends when he wanted something more?

"I am so sorry," Luke said finally.

"No, no don't be. That was why I thought tonight would be a good opportunity to get to know each other better. And I think it did, right?" He looked across at Jamie, rubbing Brick's belly, and thought back on all the fun they'd had over the night.

"Yeah, for sure." They sat in silence for a few minutes, and Luke reached over to the grab the ball and roll it across the lawn. Brick looked over and slowly rolled back onto his legs, ambling towards it. "It really was an intense night at church though. What did you think of the service and stuff?"

"It was actually pretty cool. I think it was actually a bit less intense than what I thought it would be. Like, your dad doesn't even wear robes or anything." Luke tossed up whether to tell him that his dad did, in fact, wear robes to the early morning service with the older congregation. "We went to the church back in Bulli a few times, but everyone knew my mum, so it just got a bit too much. They were really supportive, it just felt like everyone wanted to talk about her all the time and sort of join our lives. That must sound awful."

"No, I totally get it." He thought of the elderly women at the 9:30 service, who asked him almost every week whether he had a girlfriend and how things were going at school. "Like you're a celebrity or something."

"Yeah. It got super overwhelming." Jamie looked relieved that Luke understood. "So, I wasn't really sure what to expect tonight. Is it always that…"

Empty? Weird? Conservative?

"Nice?"

"Nice?" Luke echoed. "Seriously?"

"Yeah. The people were really welcoming, and I liked the way you sang about being saved, and free and stuff." So he *had* been listening. Luke cringed inwardly again at all the mistakes he had made while playing.

"Even just stopping during the service to have a cuppa and meet someone new was really, just, nice. I don't think people really do that anywhere else, like outside of churches."

"I'll pass that on to the head of welcoming." The 'head of welcoming' was, like most of the people who helped the church function, a volunteer who was just a local uni student.

"And, including Ellie, I like your family. They seem really sweet." Brick trotted back carrying the ball, and, despite the fact that Luke had thrown it, dropped it once more in Jamie's lap. He picked it up and faked throwing it far, then rolled it quietly behind a pot plant. Brick's thin tail wagged enthusiastically from side to side as he began his investigation. "Your mum's a great cook." Luke wondered if Jamie was thinking of his own mother.

"Well, we're not always that perfect, but they're an okay bunch."

"I'm glad you think so, Luke," his dad said, startling both the boys as the adults walked out. Both men were smiling, looking down at their sons sitting on the grass, the little dog sniffing around their feet. "Thank you, Jonno, for coming over tonight."

"Man, it was our pleasure, right Jamie?"

"Right," Jamie replied, grinning. "Thanks for having us over Mr Rivers." He turned to Luke, who went for a high five. Jamie wrapped his arms around him in a hug. "I'll see you at school, hey?" As they broke, Jamie gave him another of those brilliant smiles and Luke couldn't help but smile back.

4

Love stories

"Based off the theme of the day," started Ms Gander, "I thought we could practise our creative skills and write a short story about someone you love."

It was Valentine's Day, and the school had been flooded with romance.

Roses had been delivered during roll call as an initiative by the Student Representative Council, people were dropping chocolates in other people's lockers and there was more hand-holding than usual in the hallways. To his surprise, Luke had received a few roses and chocolates himself, from girls hiding behind anonymity. It was a well-known fact that Luke Rivers was single, and lesser known that he was not ready to mingle.

Most of the class groaned and Luke looked over at Jamie, sitting beside him. They had an assessment at the end of the term for creative writing, so every week, their teacher had given them a new prompt to try and get their drafts started. Mikayla attempted each one studiously, writing short stories which could each turn into something Pulitzer Prize winning. Luke, on the other hand, had attempted every writing prompt their teacher had given them without success. He usually just sat there, staring at the page and trying to come up with something, until the ten minute timer put him out of his misery. Today was different.

He found himself lost in the memory of Sunday night, sitting on the grass with Jamie. They had been watching Brick catching and returning the ball in front of them, when he had gotten so tired he had flopped on his side, still holding the ball in his mouth, tongue lolling out the side. They had both laughed so hard, something which seemed so easy when they were together. It stopped time in its tracks, that laugh.

He didn't see Jamie duck out of the room just before the timer went off.

"Okay, now I want you to swap with the person next to you and give them a bit of feedback on what they could improve."

Luke's head snapped up, but before he could stop him, the guy sitting on his other side grabbed his book.

Marcus Petrov was one of those guys who you could usually feel standing behind you, as if danger was leaking from his pores. They had been going to the same school since primary school.

Luke remembered watching him pick a little girl up once, back in Year 5, and swing her around and around on the playground. He had watched her run, sobbing, to the principal's office, hidden in reception somewhere and a terrifying place to navigate as a student. Luke didn't know whether Marcus' friends had stood up for him, or whether the school had just decided not to care, but in the end, the girl had moved schools.

He had heard she'd ended up as school captain at her new school.

Now they were on the school football team together, and every Wednesday was spent balancing his hatred of the guy with admiration for how good he was at the game.

Luke pulled Marcus' story in front of him and took as long as he could to analyse the two sentences he had written about a hot girl in the school's netball team named Sally and the day the wind had blown her tiny skirt up a bit. Marcus, apparently, thought he had fallen in love. Luke anxiously tried to study his face as he skimmed over his heart on the page.

"Man," Marcus smirked, leaning back in his chair, "this is kinda gay."

A sour metallic taste filled his mouth and he hoped he wasn't blushing. The smile Marcus was giving him seemed friendly enough but bordered on being a challenge.

"It's written from the perspective of a girl, mate, calm down." He forced a smile and grabbed his book back. "Your's wasn't Shakespearean either, sorry." The other boy pouted and pretended to wipe the tears out of his eyes.

"Know something about how a girl feels then, Luke?" Marcus asked. He forced a laughed. When the teacher looked over, Luke stuck his hand up.

"Miss, I need to go to the bathroom."

He dragged his feet along the hall to the bathroom until a teacher spotted him and asked him what he was doing out of class. The toilets were a stone's throw from the room, so he had no excuse not to head there. He closed the door behind him and walked to the sinks to splash some cold water on his face. He wondered if it would be like this forever, running from bathroom to classroom, darting from nook to cranny like some monster living in the dark, always running away. He remembered something from science about flight, fight and freeze - he was above freezing, it appeared, but wasn't a fighter either. He was just sick of flying away. Despite the water drying on his cheeks, he could feel the tears, hot and salty.

From behind him came a suffocated gasp. He wheeled around and saw, underneath the cubicle door, someone sitting on the tiled floor.

"Who's there?" he called out, wiping his face with his palms.

There was no answer, but he heard it again, this time quieter. He knew the sound well, that feeling when it feels like you're strangling yourself, when it feels like your sternum is about to pop open just to release some of the pressure. He went over and knocked on the cubicle door.

It wasn't locked, so it swung open a little and he pushed. Sitting on the floor was Jamie, one hand holding his hair back and the other shoved into a fist in his mouth. He was hunched over, shoulders shaking, face red as he leaned into the corner of the cubicle, between the toilet and the wall, trying to take up as little space as possible.

Trying to disappear.

"Hey, are you okay?" Luke crouched down to look him in the eye. The other boy shook his head, almost imperceptibly. He sank to the floor, back against the wall too, and hesitated before resting a hand on his knee. They both looked at it, but neither boy made an attempt to move it. "What happened?" The other boy tried to answer but could only produce a hiccup. Luke tried to remember something from his first aid course. "Try and, uh, take deep breaths."

Jamie closed his eyes and tilted his head back, as if trying to let something trapped escape from his throat. "I just," he began before his breath snagged.

He shook his head and tried again.

"When Miss asked us to write about someone we love, I started writing about my dad," he said, looking at the ceiling.

He wrapped his arms around his knees, interlocking his fingers until the knuckles turned white.

"I started writing about him, and growing up and stuff, and how we used to go and get fish and chips after a surf sometimes. I used to love doing that with him, and it was special, our little secret."

Luke imagined a smaller version of Jamie, trying to balance a surfboard under his arm, still dripping in his wetsuit and sand on his eyelashes.

"But that got me thinking about how, when we'd get home, stuffed with fish, mum would always have made spag bol, because she knew it was my favourite and I couldn't resist, and I would scarf it down anyway, because I couldn't believe I was so… lucky." His words came out all jumbled, trying to get the words out as quickly as possible before he couldn't anymore. "You know, lucky that I got both my favourite foods and my favourite people."

Luke looked up to see Jamie let a tear roll down his cheek. "I'm really sorry."

Jamie waved the words away. "It's not like it's your fault." He stretched out a leg, pressing it against the other wall of the cubicle. "I just don't know how it's ever going to feel better." His voice broke again and he looked away, rubbing angrily at his eyes.

"Yeah," Luke forced himself to look down at his hands. "It must be hard, to lose your mum."

"She was the best," Jamie whispered, mostly to himself.

"What was she like?" Luke asked, quickly adding, "you don't have to answer if you don't want." But Jamie answered as though he hadn't heard.

"She was kind. So, so loving. Like, whoever came to the house always felt welcomed and she had this way of making conversation with anyone. She would always have made something for them to eat, and I guess it kind of lulled them into a sense of security, but it also felt like she always had all the time in the world just to hear you. Made you feel really special." He rested his head against the wall, lost in his own memories. "And she was also a really good cook. I think she wanted to open a restaurant at some point, and dad was always telling her that she would have been able to. She was one of those people who would know just what a dish needed by tasting it, didn't even need a recipe. My dad burns toast." They both laughed and Luke pressed his shoulder against Jamie's.

They sat there, on the bathroom floor, in silence for a few minutes. He was conscious of their skin touching at the elbow, the breathing of the other boy as it slowed and that smell again, distinctive above the scent of the bathroom.

"She sounds really special," Luke said eventually. "I wish I had gotten the chance to meet her."

"She always used to say that I'd see her again soon," Jamie whispered. "That sounds so silly, but I believed her."

"Like, in heaven?"

"Yeah, she really believed in all that. I guess that's why we started going to church, to sort of understand it for ourselves. I wish I had gone with her a bit more when she was around."

"I've never thought about it like that before, heaven," Luke replied. When he looked up, he was staring directly into Jamie's sky blue eyes. They were as clear as sea glass.

Luke was trying to think of something else to say when the bell rang.

"Man, sorry I've been rambling so long," Jamie said, as Luke stood, reaching out a hand to pull him up. "Thanks for listening."

"No, it was really cool getting to know you better." Luke brushed his hands against his shorts. "And I am sorry, about your mum. If you ever want to talk more, I'd be happy to listen."

"Thanks, man," Jamie smiled, holding the door of the stall open for him with a flourish, as if they weren't in the dingy boy's toilets, but about to step into a fancy restaurant. He couldn't help but grin back, the weight of their combined sadness slowly dissipating.

They walked back to class together and snuck into the back to grab their backpacks as everyone else was heading out.

***

Mikayla couldn't believe her eyes when Jamie walked over with Luke at lunch and sat down to eat his sandwich.

"Careful Mickey, if the wind changes direction, your face will be stuck like that."

"Don't call me Mickey," she hissed at Luke and opened up a flask of massaman curry. "Hey," she said, shifting her tone and smiling winsomely. It was like watching a caterpillar turn into a butterfly. "What's your name?"

Jamie reached out a hand for her to shake and introduced himself. Luke rolled his eyes. "My name is Jamie, I'm new here this term."

"Oh really?" she fluttered her lashes like black wings.

"Yeah, I think I'm in your art class and I was in your English class today…" He glanced over at Luke and they both smiled. "At least, I was for a bit."

Mikayla stared at Luke suspiciously, as if he was guilty of keeping some inside joke from her. In a way he was, he realised; he hadn't been about to tell her what Jamie had shared in the bathroom. Secrets were rare in their relationship but hey, he was already keeping a pretty big one. What was one more?

"Well, I get alright grades if you ever need some help," she said finally. Luke snorted- Mikayla was the top of the class. She would be getting 101% if it were possible. Noticing the way she was glaring at him, he pretended he had something stuck in his throat.

"Thanks, I'll let you know if I ever need some help. Whereabouts are you from, Mickey?" This time, he couldn't help it. Luke snorted and the two boys cracked up.

"My name, *Jamie*," she put particular emphasis on the two syllables of his name, as if she were about to issue an afternoon detention, "is Mikayla, whatever this literal *feral* may have told you." That set the boys off again and Mikayla deflated, wiping the sides of her flask with a naan.

"Sorry, sorry," Jamie said, pulling out his sandwich. From the looks of it, they both had Vegemite, Luke noted. "Genuinely, tell me a bit about yourself Mikayla. I didn't see you on Friday?"

What's on Friday? Mikayla mouthed to Luke, who mouthed back, *youth group.* Her eyes widened with realisation.

"Oh, I don't usually go to Luke's church," she replied. "I tend to be really busy studying and, like, volunteering as well." Luke rolled his eyes.

"I happen to volunteer at the same time and place as you, Mi-kay-la," he said, purposely drawing out every syllable of her name, "and I know it's on a Wednesday. You've always got plenty of time on Friday afternoons." Maybe Jamie could finally get her through the door.

"I do study *sometimes*," she narrowed her eyes at him.

"I wouldn't want to disturb your busy *schedule*, then!" Luke poked out his tongue at her. Jamie's eyes were flitting from one friend to another as though he were watching a ping pong match.

"What do you guys volunteer for?" Jamie finally interjected, and Mikayla launched into an explanation of the program they were a part of.

"It's probably too late for you to finish it, but you might be able to get a bronze medal," she finished.

"Even without the medal, I reckon it's worth it," Luke added, thinking of Fuddy. "I mean, hanging out with a bunch of senior citizens isn't always my idea of a good time, but it's definitely more interesting than picking up trash like Daniel." Their friend Daniel had started his acts of service by playing a game on the internet where every correct answer on a quiz was guaranteed to collect him 10 grains of rice for a starving child in Africa. However, once their teacher had found out, she had convinced Daniel that, in fact, most charity workers had better things to do with their time than count out grains of rice, and he had been asked to change the volunteer portion of the program.

"Come with us," Mikayla gently nudged him on the arm.

So, that Wednesday, the three of them headed back with their school group to the nursing home.

As Luke walked in, flanked by Mikayla and Jamie, he was pleased to see Fuddy in the same chair, waving to them. The three of them went over to say hello.

"We've heard a lot about you, Mr Richards," Mikayla said, reaching out her hand. He took it and gently kissed the top.

"You must be Mikayla," he said, in that same gentle whisper, and she flushed, pleased to have been the mentioned in conversation. "And you are?" The old man looked over to Jamie, and Luke rushed forward to introduce him.

"This is Jamie, he's new. We've convinced him to join the program." The words were tumbling out of his mouth almost faster than he could form them, and he took a deep breath to calm his nerves. Fuddy was the first person he had formally introduced Jamie to, and it felt almost momentous.

"It is a pleasure to meet you Jamie," Fuddy replied, shaking Jamie's hand firmly.

"Oh, you too, sir. You're practically the only reason Luke wanted to come back today, I reckon." He laughed and Luke punched him playfully on the arm.

"Please, call me Fuddy. Or Elmer, if you must be formal."

"I really like what you're wearing, Elmer," Mikayla said, gesturing to his outfit. He was wearing a wine coloured tie today with a velvet dinner jacket, piped in black.

"Ah, thank you my dear. You never know when you'll be going some-where special or entertaining guests." As true as it was, no one else around them seemed to mind their appearance much. His clothes set him apart from everyone else in the nursing home, including the nurses, who were all dressed as though they had been left out in the sun too long.

Luke sat opposite Fuddy as the teacher called Mikayla over to the same old woman waiting for her as last week and Jamie was paired with an old man who looked like he was staring intently at something invisible in the corner. The old man pushed a chessboard on a little side table with wheels between them.

"So, how has your week been, Luke?" Fuddy asked as he began sorting out the pieces into black and white piles. Luke pulled the black pieces towards himself and started setting up the board.

"It's actually been a pretty hectic time," he replied.

"Is that good? Bad?"

Luke mulled it over. "Both, I think." He told Fuddy about Jamie being at youth group and church, and the awkward family dinner.

"It sounds like a lot of this week has had to do with Jamie," the old man smiled. "He sounds like he's becoming a good friend."

"He is, I guess." Luke looked over to the other boy, who was trying to talk to his nursing home patient and looking as though he would rather be speaking to a brick wall.

"What is he like?"

"Jamie?" The old man nodded.

Luke started to list off all of the things he had found out about or really liked about Jamie from the past week and found that there was an almost endless list.

After listening for a few minutes and sitting in thought, Fuddy said, "Sometimes we just need people like that in our lives. New friends to come along, just at the right moment."

"Yeah," Luke said, setting up his pieces. "Ready for a rematch?"

That afternoon, they talked again like they were old friends who had known each other for a long time. Fuddy shared memories of growing up after World War II and how soldiers had been poorly received returning from Vietnam. Fuddy and his brother had been conscripted, and his brother hadn't returned, which made being vilified by the public even harder.

"I had initially wanted to be a conscientious objector," Fuddy told Luke, "but in the end decided it was more helpful if I actually went and helped these guys process what was going on around them, so I went as an army chaplain. Most of the time, people just wanted someone to talk to, but occasionally I would hold a funeral service or pray with someone as they were on their deathbed." Luke tried to imagine the man in front of him as only a few years older than himself. "Those are the moments that still stick with me, all these years later - the stench of death was just so thick everywhere you went. To come home and be treated like you hadn't really done your duty somehow, that was really tough on a lot of the men who returned. After we came home, a lot of men never really spoke about what they had gone through with anyone, and it ate them up from the inside out."

Fuddy's voice, as breathy as Luke remembered it being from the week before, was quiet and gentle, even as he spoke passionately about his past. The room was one of the only places he knew which could be so quiet while filled with so many people.

"What made you want to be a chaplain?" Luke asked.

"Faith is a powerful tool, Luke, no matter what you're believing in. I would prefer to put my trust in a God who says he has a plan, and is watching out for me, but some people just need to know that there's something bigger out there than themselves."

"How long have you been a Christian?"

"I grew up with a Christian family, much like yourself," Fuddy asked, moving one of the pieces on his side of the board, "but I think there is a time when every young person has to decide for themselves they are going to own what they believe, or it's not really theirs." Luke's brow furrowed as he mulled this over.

"How did you know that's what you wanted for yourself?"

"I can tell you how I knew, but I can't tell you how you will know, if that's what you're asking." The old man glanced up with a twinkle in his eye.

"Okay, so how did *you* know?"

"I was just a bit older than you, away from my family for the first time at university, and I realised just how free I was. I started dating, and partying, but it felt empty at the end of the day. One night, I was pulled over by some police officers with my drunk friends in the back and I was frankly embarrassed by them. What's worse is that, on other nights, I had been just like them, with some other schmuck driving *me* home." Luke tried to imagine the man in front of him as a teenager and struggled. "So, I tried to figure out what was missing and the only thing which had really changed since the beginning of university was that I had stopped acting out my faith. Once I picked it up again, things went back to feeling normal - not just normal, but better. Since then, every time I have had that unsettled or painful feeling, returning to the cross has brought that peace back."

"Do you think you would have felt that way if you hadn't grown up in a Christian family?"

"Oh, definitely," Fuddy replied immediately. "I have been all over the world since then and met many people who had never even heard the gospel before. Many of them have left their families, their homes, given up huge parts of themselves to follow Christ. It changes you Luke, if you'll let it. Jesus promised that there would be more to life than this present world

- in John, he says 'in this world, you will have trouble, but take heart, for I have overcome the world.' The trouble part, we know instinctively to be true, but I have also found the latter half to be true, when I let Christ be my guide." Luke could feel Fuddy studying his face as he sat, deep in thought. "Is something troubling you?"

He thought back over the past week and how good it had been, just getting to know Jamie. He felt like he had been waiting for the other shoe to drop. "No," he replied, looking over at the other boy again. "At least, not yet."

Fuddy slapped his hands on his knees and the sound startled Luke out of his thoughts. "That looks like checkmate, by the way." Luke had been so engrossed in what Fuddy was saying that he had barely paid attention to the moves he was making. He looked down at the board and fell back in his chair.

"How do you do it?"

"I think part of it might be about distracting your opponent, but that's not going to do you any favours if you're ever in an actual tournament, so we'll have to continue our lessons next week." The old man smiled, gesturing at the students starting to gather at the doors.

"Thanks, Fuddy."

"Thank you, Luke," the old man replied.

***

The three walked out into the warm air, barely starting to contain the cooler breeze that autumn would bring.

"How was that?" Luke asked his friends, as they walked side by side on the footpath. He knew from experience that if it got too narrow, he would be expected to drop behind, but for now, he was just enjoying being in the middle.

Mikayla groaned. "This week the topic was how we're all wasting our money on buying smashed avo on toast instead of saving up for home loans. Isn't that the whole reason you get a *loan*? Because you can't afford the house anyway?"

Jamie shrugged. "I don't know anything about home loans, and I don't know anything about old people, but I think either the guy I was talking to was in a coma or he was pretending to be so I would go away."

"Sheesh, you guys really drew the short straws."

"Don't you dare talk about Elmer, and how he was so lovely, and how he taught you chess," Mikayla grumbled.

"He's teaching you chess?" Jamie raised an eyebrow.

"Yes," she snapped, "and probably lets him drink tea and eat biscuits without complaining about how the *decadence* of the *youth* is spoiling the economy!" She vehemently spat the words out as she walked along.

"Well I can't help that your lady seems to hate you, but yeah, Elmer is actually really lovely."

"What do you guys talk about?" Jamie asked.

"I don't know, everything. Nothing. Today we just kind of talked about how he went to war and became a Christian, and, well, you guys."

"What did you say about us?" Mikayla asked, her attention temporarily diverted from her afternoon rant.

"I don't know," Luke blushed, feeling his face heat up to the same colour as his bright copper hair. "Just what my week was like and how things are going with you guys. He's got some good advice, you know?"

"On what, exactly, Lucas Rivers?" She stopped and put her hands on her hips.

"On how to deal with pests like you, Mikayla Norma McNamara," he retorted, poking her gently in the side.

"Hey guys, wait a second," Jamie said, and the three of them stopped on the path. He had a serious look on his face, his brow furrowed and his mouth straight. "Mickey's initials are M'n'M!" Mikayla groaned and stomped off while the two boys high fived and jogged to catch up with her. They danced around her until she cracked up laughing and the three of them collapsed onto the steps of the church, pushing, joking and giggling.

That afternoon was the first time Luke realised they fit together.

Not three strangers trying to figure each other out or two and a spare, but a group.

And it felt wonderful.

5
Fetch

For the next few days at school, the three of them would find each other after school to sit together.

It felt like his little unit with Mikayla had grown a little bit, and that was a good thing - he finally had another guy to talk to, and she could fawn over Jamie as much as she liked while actually getting to know him better. Jamie had even started taking the empty seat next to Luke in classes without her around.

It was both exciting and exhausting at the same time, always keeping a filter on so he didn't do or say anything stupid. Conversations about the formal or gossip about who was dating whom in the school were especially tricky, as they usually swung around to talking about the three of them, Mikayla making not-so-subtle hints at Jamie that she was waiting for him to make the first move and Luke sitting to the side like the third wheel on a bicycle.

He found himself thinking about Jamie when they weren't together as well.

At one point, Ellie had found him reading one of her magazines, hunched over it at his desk. She had come into his room to find a pair of scissors and, typically Ellie, hadn't bothered to knock.

"What are you doing with that?" she had asked, innocuously spinning the scissors around her forefinger.

"They don't make this kind of magazine for boys," he had replied defensively, flipping it shut. He had been doing a multiple choice quiz called 'Does he want to kiss, kill or avoid you?' The verdict had been pretty dire.

"Right." She drew the word out so that it sounded about ten syllables instead of one. "It looks like she's just not that into you," she had giggled, spinning on her heels and flipping her long blonde ponytail behind her.

He had wondered, after she left, whether she would have made a good confidante, whether she would have actually been really happy for him. Like hard boiling an egg, the worst thing about the wrong thing to say is that you don't know it's wrong until you've said it.

The news was clearly spreading around the school that Jamie had joined their group as well. One morning, Stacey Williams had come up to him during roll call.

"Hey Luke, would you be free on the 22nd of March by any chance?"

Stacey was a girl in his Maths class who knew the answer to every question. He liked sitting next to her because the teacher purposely didn't look their way when asking questions in an attempt to give someone else a chance.

"Yeah, maybe." The 22nd of March was the weekend before the end of school. It was next month, and Luke didn't even know what he was doing next weekend. "Why?"

"I'm having a little get together at my house, nothing major." She gave him a big grin, whipping a light purple envelope out of her bag with his name on the front in big, loopy writing. "I hope to see you there." He gave her a feeble smile - the envelope smelled like flowers. Just as she went to walk away and he went to release the breath he had been holding, she swung back around on the heel of her shoe. "Oh, and if you could see if Jamie is available, I'd be happy for him to come along."

"Oh, okay. Is it okay if I bring my friend Mikayla?" he asked before she turned away again.

She paused and he could see her weighing up the pros and cons. "If it means you'll be there, sure."

She gave him that broad grin again and walked off, her plaits swinging left and right with her steps.

At recess, Luke brought it up with his friends.

"Oh my gosh, I had heard that something was going down this week-end." Mikayla's eyes nearly popped out of her head. "Our first real high school party, and not a second too soon as well."

Jamie and Luke glanced at each other over their friend's excitement, both struggling to hold back giggles.

"Surely you've been to a party before?" Jamie asked, pulling bits of crust off his sandwich to chuck to nearby pigeons.

Mikayla looked at him, her eyes still worryingly wide. "Yes, James, but those have been *kid's* parties. Like, pinatas and pass the parcel sort of dos. This is a real, teenage party, with boys and girls and *no parents*. Oh gosh, what are we going to wear?" She was almost immediately lost to them again, mentally sorting through her wardrobe for something even mildly appropriate while chewing on a date. Luke didn't want to tell her that he had, in fact, been invited to a few parties before, but hadn't wanted to go without her. There had only been a few get-togethers after football games and even those, he hadn't told her about.

"I'll try to keep my nice jeans out of the wash," Luke joked. Mikayla glared at him.

"You guys are hopeless." Jamie tried to protest, but gave up.

"Get some girl friends then," Luke retorted.

She scoffed. "You wish, jerk-bag." She smiled and threw a seed at him. He dodged and grabbed one from her lunch box. "Wanna date, Jamie?" Mikayla asked, cocking her head to the side innocently. He laughed and grabbed one for himself.

"Sure, Mickey. I'd love one."

Luke and Mikayla both felt the colour rush to their face.

***

On the Friday afternoon at lunch, the three of them had just sat down in the quad when there was a shout from behind them.

Over on the other side of the quad, a group of younger boys were playing handball in a grid, replacing each other when someone got out. The yell had come from a scrawny boy, who could only have been in year 7. Marcus Petrov was holding a yellow rubber ball above his head as he jumped and reached out for it.

"Give it back, that's not yours!" The kid's voice was high pitched and squeaky with anxiety, which only made Marcus and his friends laugh even more. His friends were looking around anxiously for a teacher or some-one who could help. Before he could overthink it, Luke stood up and walked over.

"Give it back." He was surprised at how level his voice sounded, con-sidering he was standing alone.

"Come on Lukey, don't you want to play piggy in the middle?" He threw the ball casually to one of his mates, an empty-headed buffoon called Taylor (Tricky, to those who knew him well), who started tossing it around to other boys, laughing like a circus seal. "Your girlfriend's watching."

Luke turned around and saw that indeed, Mikayla was standing up and observing anxiously.

So was Jamie.

"You need to start picking on people your own size, Marcus. I know that sort of person might be hard to find," he couldn't help adding. Even though both boys were captains of the team, they were built differently. Luke was tall and slender, usually a winger who had to be quick and lithe. Marcus, however, was usually in the middle of the field, ready to grab the ball and charge, like a bull, from one end to the other. There were a few boys who got together to play tackle on the oval at lunch when the teachers weren't looking - that was his *true* speciality, when it didn't matter if someone was fast enough to tag him but dumb enough to try and take him down.

"I'm sure little Freddy here can handle himself," Marcus said, hitting the kid on the back so hard he stumbled forward and smiling in a way which didn't quite reach his eyes.

"Give him back the ball, Marcus." Luke glanced over at the smaller boys, staring up at him with a mixture of anticipation and admiration. Even though he felt anxious, his voice betrayed no sign of a tremor. Someone threw the ball back to him and his grip tightened around it.

"Fine," he answered, his mirthless smile widening. "Come on, puppy dog." Marcus flung back his arm. "Fetch." He threw the ball as hard as he could, everyone watching it fly to the other side of the quad. The little blonde boy who had been jumping before started to run in its direction, but a hand reached up and pulled it out of the air with ease. Jamie was standing on the other side of the quad, clutching the ball and he threw it, just as hard, all the way back to Luke.

He smiled and handed the ball back to the younger boys, but as Marcus turned away, he could have sworn he heard him mutter under his breath, 'There's something going on there.'

"That was so stupid of you, Luke!" Mikayla admonished him as soon as he was within earshot.

"Brave, mate, she means brave." Jamie gave him a small punch on the arm. "That guy seems like he's got a few screws loose."

"You don't know the half of it. I have to play footy with the guy," Luke replied, thinking about how awkward the next match would be, when they would be co-captains again. "That was a pretty impressive catch though, you should think about trying out for the team."

"I used to help my dad bowl for his cricket matches, but it's nice to know I've still got that muscle memory in case I ever need it."

The three settled down again in the shade, watching the younger boys resume their game of handball. It felt good to know he had helped, but he couldn't help turning over what he thought Marcus had said in his mind. A Bible verse came to him, not from a sermon or study but a Stephen King novel about drug dealers in a small town - 'the guilty man flees where none pursueth'. He wondered how he would have to pay for standing up to Marcus in the future.

6
Waves

The hands had been moving around the clock for hours now. They were literal hands, a blown-up image of a cartoon dog spinning round and round, keeping track of the seconds and minutes in Jamie's house. The clock was seated atop a tv cabinet, the shelves either side filled to the brim with photographs. The room was empty other than an old couch, a small wooden sideboard and the dining table they were seated at. It was small, but Jamie's dad had worked hard to make it feel like a home.

The boys were wasting their Saturday trying to help each other figure out what to do for their final Modern History project.

"It just has to be a person of historical significance," Luke said for the billionth time.

"I literally don't even think I could say those words right now. His… History… Hysterical…"

The two boys laughed and Jamie went to refill their glasses with iced water. It was a scorcher outside, so hot that Luke could feel the sweat dripping down the back of his knees.

"I was thinking of doing some sort of Christian hero, someone who has done something important for the community in the past hundred years." Luke was pretty sure he had said that exact same sentence before as well, based on the tabs which he had opened in the first ten minutes of their study session and hadn't touched since. He had spent the rest of the time staring at the same sentences in the book or pausing to tell Jamie something interesting or funny. A lot of that time had just been trying to beat each other's high scores in Space Invader.

"What about that guy in the youth talk last night? Martin Luther King?"

"Just Martin Luther," Luke corrected absentmindedly. Mikayla had made another last minute excuse while Luke had walked home with her. Jamie caught the bus, and it almost felt like when she wasn't in his presence, the allure of coming to church had worn off.

"I genuinely don't think I can do any more right now," Jamie said, placing their glasses on the table. The ice he had put in them had already half disappeared.

"I'm glad you said it, because neither can I." He leaned back in his chair, feeling the weak breeze from a rotating fan on the back of his neck.

"Let's hit the beach then!" Jamie's enthusiasm seemed foreign in the lazy quiet of the afternoon.

Luke could see the heat radiating in waves off the road outside and, just a few kilometres beyond it, the dark blue horizon of the beach. Despite the size of the Rivers' apartment, you could see the azure of the sea from their window. The sun was shining, the sky was clear, and they were inside trying to study - it had been a plan doomed from the start.

"I should probably try and absorb some of this... You go if you want, and we can try again at school."

"It's like, three thirty, mate," Jamie replied, and looked up at Goofy. Luke could swear the clock was moving in slow motion. The house was so quiet, he felt like he could hear his own heartbeat in his ears.

He swallowed, his tongue sticking to the top of his dry mouth. "Okay, then."

Luke wandered down the brick steps to wait for his friend outside, and noticed that the footpath was littered with garbage. It looked like people had come from kilometres around to dump their old couches, stained mattresses, broken chairs and half empty buckets of paint. 'It is junk', they were saying to the people living in the Department housing, 'and so are you'.

Luke took a seat on the low brick fence and thought about going to the beach together. He couldn't stop his knee from jittering as he tried to sit still - it was as though his body was simultaneously telling him to do this and not to do this.

"Ready?" Jamie bounded down the footpath, shaking Luke from his reverie. His hair was pulled to the back of his head in a little bun, and he had changed into a faded blue sleeveless shirt which brought out the cool blue of his eyes. The soles of his sneakers flapped up from the ground a second after his feet did and Luke smiled up at him, feeling the anxiety slowly drift away. "Aren't you hot?"

Luke was caught off guard for a second before his brain registered the question. He was wearing all black, from his cap to his sneakers, and he could feel the sun sucking the moisture from his shoulders through the weight of his thick cotton shirt.

"Nah, she'll be right mate." With that, both boys turned towards the beach.

As they walked down the hill, Luke bounced a football against the path on its point, watching as it spun back up towards him. Red haired and freckled, his ancestors had spent the past two hundred years trying to adjust to the Australian heat, especially in summer. Even layers of sunscreen couldn't last the recommended two hours before reapplication – if he didn't want to get burned, he had to cover himself head to toe. He could tell his pale skin was already starting to turn pink, bringing out his freckles.

Cars with surfboards tied to their roofs whizzed by as a blue bus chugged its way, slowly but surely, towards the peak.

"I just want to say, I'm sorry you were paired with me- I'm supposed to be helping you figure your assignment out and I haven't got a clue about my own."

Jamie laughed. "I've got a few ideas, but I haven't actually started writing anything yet. Kowalski wants a draft by the end of term." Their history teacher was an old Polish man, who had lived through some of the things he was teaching about. Famously, he had met the biographer for Hitler's cinematographer, Leni Riefenstahl, and shaken his hand. That man had met the woman who had shaken Hitler's hand and so, Mr Kowalski had shaken hands with Hitler with only three degrees of separation. Also famously, Mr Kowalski hadn't changed his teaching methods since he got his diploma in the 80's.

"What topics were you thinking about?" Luke asked, bouncing the football down and watching as it came back into his hands.

The beach was split in half by the fish and chip shop in the middle. On one side, all of the families had gathered near the red and yellow flags, little kids splashing under the watchful eye of the lifeguards. Seagulls stood on the stone steps, their eager eyes waiting to swoop towards a dropped chip or away from a small child, ambling amongst the sunbathers turning like rotisserie chickens.

"Do you mind if we don't talk about school for a bit?" Jamie asked. Tall pine trees provided shade for them along the path, which slowly turned from concrete, to metal grates, to sand. "I just need a break."

"Yeah sure, we don't have to talk about school."

The other side of the beach was quieter, where the waves weren't as high and there weren't many surfers or families at all, just the occasional paddler or professional swimmer, their long, rhythmic strokes slicing through the water.

"Ever surfed?" Luke asked.

"Yeah, a tiny bit. There aren't great waves where I'm from, so you'd usually have to wait for the perfect day. Sometimes, it felt like literally everyone was down at the beach, waiting to catch a wave, even if it meant missing school."

"Those days are the best." Luke thought of one afternoon a few years ago, when his dad had brought him and Ellie down to the beach and they hadn't even been able to find a few metres to put a towel and their stuff. He remembered watching his dad crouch down, the curl of the wave skimming his tall figure, and thinking (for the first time in a long time) that his dad was actually a bit cool. "That's what I want to do once this is all over – go somewhere that's just perfect waves, day after day."

"After school?"

"Yeah." Luke hadn't really thought of what he was going to do in the interim after he had finished his HSC. It had always seemed so far away, but he realised with a start that it was only a few months now. "Somewhere on the beach, just a few friends and a board, eating fish and chips every day." He smiled at the thought.

"That sounds perfect – I'll bring the sunscreen, you bring the wax." Luke realised Jamie had somehow included himself in the plan and was now imagining the two of them, slicing through the water on some tropical island.

"What are you going to do next year?" he asked, just to distract himself.

Holding their shoes in their hands, they turned away from the people towards the more secluded south side of the beach to kick the ball around. Luke gently chucked the ball to Jamie and threw his shoes onto the tiny purple flowers dotted along where the grass met the golden sand. It was burning hot on his soles, but his muscles relaxed as the wind puddled the sand around his feet.

Jamie laughed. "Write more essays, probably. I want to do something with literature or journalism - English is about the only subject I'm good at."

He pulled off his shirt to reveal a tanned, muscular torso. His arms were long and lean, strong without looking like he purposely worked on them. Luke knew he had made the swimming team as soon as he had tried out for it and it was unusual for them to let someone in after the official tryouts in the first week of school. He found himself tracing the curve of his shoulders, the toned creases in his abdomen, before forcing himself to look away.

He hoped that the redness of his face would be chalked up to the heat, and started studying the sand.

"How about you?" Jamie asked, seemingly oblivious. He kicked the ball to Luke, skimming it across the mini hills and valleys in the sand like a pebble.

Every time Luke tried to imagine the year after school, it was like looking into a black hole.

"I dunno yet," he said, forcing himself to focus on the ball. "Somehow the conversation has come back to school. What else is going on for you?"

He looked up and could have sworn that Jamie was blushing. "Well, I've kind of been thinking about Mikayla." He picked up the ball and threw it to Luke, who jogged backwards a few steps to catch it. "What do you think of her?" Jamie asked, scratching the back of his head, jostling a few strands of hair out of his bun so that they fell to frame his face.

"Well, she *is* my best friend," Luke replied.

Of course this was where it was going to go. As if he hadn't seen them getting closer over the past few days, laughing when he joined them for lunch, already in the middle of conversation when he walked into the room. He knew she liked Jamie - he had known that since Jamie had started at their school - but maybe a selfish part of him had been hoping that Jamie wouldn't have to like her back, at least for a little bit.

"She's awesome, though, and I think she likes you."

"Oh, really?" Luke could tell he was trying to downplay his excitement, but he looked pleased.

"Why, were you thinking of asking her out?" He kicked the ball back.

"I don't want to get in your way or anything, if you guys have a thing going," the words tumbled out of Jamie's mouth and Luke's heart sank. He was always so quick to be kind, to try and do the right thing.

"No, we're just friends," he smiled as convincingly as he could, knowing it hadn't reached his eyes but hoping they were far enough apart that it wouldn't matter. Jamie kicked the ball and it shot right past him, soaring into the water.

"Sorry!" he called out as Luke turned and ran into the water.

Even though they were only a few minutes away from the main beach, there was no one around. As he waded into the water, all he could hear was the crash of the waves being pulled in with the tide, the sand turning from burning hot to cold under his feet as he got closer to the water, the trickle of the ocean between his toes. He relished the silence as the water slowly washed mounds of wet sand over his feet, the suction as he pulled his feet up to trudge slowly deeper and deeper, until it came up to his waist. A shiver ran up his spine as the water pooled and he took a deep breath. He plunged his head underneath. For a second, there was total silence.

Of course that was how it was going to go.

He watched as bubbles burst from all around him, rushing up to meet the air.

You're just dragging them down.

He held himself under the water as long as he could, watching a wave form above him, pulling water around it to make a smooth curl like a lock of blue-green crystal hair, watched as it rushed towards the shore and collapsed in on itself. His eyes burned with the salt water.

They don't even need you around any more.

He could see feet wading towards him, causing bursts of sand to explode from the seabed as they came nearer. Luke pushed his feet up against the ocean floor and stood up, to see Jamie making his way over, catching the ball with one arm as it floated by.

"Is everything okay, man?"

Luke breathed in the clear air and smoothed his hair out of his face, feeling the sun almost immediately drying his shoulders and back.

"Yeah, of course," he clapped his friend on the shoulder as they walked back to shore, "except that you're going to get a sunburn if you don't put on a shirt soon." The two walked back to the beach, side by side, and, despite the fact that Jamie was already a deep olive tan, Luke watched as his friend pulled his shirt back over his head before throwing the ball back to him.

Of course that was going to happen.

***

That afternoon as they headed home, dark clouds started to gather overhead. It felt like walking through jelly.

They had spent the afternoon tossing the ball around before heading up to the shops to get some ice cream, Jamie with chocolate and Luke strawberry gelato. For hours, they had watched as the sun descended behind them, casting gold glitter on the water. They had tried to guess who people were as they watched, just from how they talked or what they did at the beach. Old men in speedos who didn't care if anyone was watching, self-conscious teenage girls and giggling kids running through the seagulls. Luke had wondered what people would say if they saw him and Jamie, sitting on the steps.

It had sucked saying goodbye, but Jamie had promised his dad that he would be home for dinner, so Luke hopped on a bus and ran through the day in his head. He had realised with a start that he hadn't told anyone he was heading out - hadn't even left a note - but there were no missed calls or unanswered texts on his phone. It had felt good just to be in Jamie's company, just the two of them, no one looking over his shoulder.

He ran inside as it started to sprinkle and dropped his backpack by the front door, kicking his shoes off onto the porch where they could spill sand everywhere. He ran a hand through his hair, feeling the skin starting to peel near the base of his neck. That was going to hurt like hell tomorrow, he thought absentmindedly, wandering into the kitchen for a drink. His mum was at the sink, cutting up vegetables for dinner.

"Well, it's nice to finally see you!" she joked, dropping a freshly peeled potato into a bowl of water. "Where have you been all day, mister?"

"Just hanging out with a friend," he said, reaching around her to fill a glass with water.

"Mickey?" His mum raised an eyebrow.

"No," he hesitated. "A different friend." His mum had been waiting for him and Mickey to get together since they were in primary school. He didn't know how to break it to her that that was probably not going to happen, least of all with Jamie now in the picture.

"Ooh, a girl?" his mum stopped to size him up, a coy look in her eye.

"No," he said, surprising himself with the hard note in his voice. "Jamie, who you met on Sunday. We're in Modern History together and we've got a project we're supposed to be working on." He skulled his water as quickly as he could, trying to escape her stare. Why couldn't she just let it be?

"Oh, I'm sorry," she poked him gently in the ribs with the top of the potato peeler. "I just thought you had a cheeky grin on your face when you walked through the door." She turned back to her potatoes, and Luke felt his heart sink. She would have been over the moon if he had been out with a girl. The thought crossed his mind that maybe he should have lied, but what would have been the point? It would never be true. "Speaking of Mikayla, have you heard anything about the formal coming up at the end of the year? She might be someone you could take. Unless there's someone else on your mind." Luke could hear thunder in the distance. The rain started to suck all the air from the room and he could feel himself start to break into a sweat.

"I was thinking of going by myself," he mumbled, then added, "or I might see if Jamie wants to go with me. We could go with Mikayla as a group."

"A group of you?" It sounded like there were a few questions packed into one.

He could see the formal so clearly in his mind as his mum imagined it.

The picture had gone from a smiling Luke, in his new suit and tie, arm supporting some beauty teetering in her heels, to the three of them, awkwardly shoved in the back seat of a taxi together.

Suddenly, his two friends vanished and Luke pictured himself sitting alone.

Outside, lightning flashed and hard bullets of rain started to rattle on the tin roof over the veranda.

"You sure there isn't a nice girl in your class you could ask?"

The picture in Luke's mind of him in his formal suit turned into one of him graduating university, alone.

Getting his first job and trying to tell his mum at Christmas lunch, only to be asked when she would be getting some grandkids.

Buying a house, and everyone's snide digs about it being a bachelor's pad.

"Why do you always have to be on my back about girls, mum?" It had started as a plea and ended as a shout. She looked up just long enough for him to see the shock on her face - the realisation? - as he grabbed his helmet and headed back out into the storm.

He started cycling down the hill, not paying any attention to the streets around him. The footpath was mostly empty, people scurrying into their apartments and houses with bright umbrellas breaking up the grey.

He used to go to his mum with everything. Every scrape and bruise, every complaint, especially against Ellie. When had that all stopped?

He almost swerved in front of a dark grey car, its headlights dim in the thick veil of rain. It blared its horn at him and he rolled back onto the footpath, jabbing the button until the pedestrian light went green. He passed the park where he used to have soccer practice, and the street he would have walked down with his dad to primary school.

She was there when he got the scar on his forearm playing handball, and had been the first to the hospital when he had broken that same arm playing basketball. She had known him since he was born, but it was like she didn't even know him at all these days.

His shirt was sticking to his back as he struggled to see where he was going. He pedalled furiously, his feet trying to outpace his heartbeat, trying to release some of the anxiety that was building in his blood. He rolled down the ramp on the corner of a street and looked left and right as he crossed.

The worst part was, she would love Jamie.

Luke aimed for the ramp up on the other side, squinting for the gap in the grey concrete. A car pulled out of a driveway and surprised him, causing him to jerk his handlebars swiftly to the left. He felt his front wheel jar to a stop while the back wheel spun out of control as he fell onto the concrete.

Blood mixing with the water running down into the drain, he wept.

***

When Mikayla opened the door, she gasped. Her mother poked her head out to see who had rung the bell and immediately disappeared to grab a towel and put the kettle on. Having grown up in London, she knew there were some things which could only be fixed with a cuppa.

Mikayla grabbed the first aid kit out of the kitchen cupboard as her mum bustled around, measuring tea leaves into strainers which looked like deep sea divers and puppy dogs. She took another look at Luke, dripping onto her black and white tiles, and added honey for good measure.

"What the hell happened?" His friend poured some foul maroon liquid onto a cotton swab and started dabbing at the deep gashes on his knees and forearms. As gentle as she was being, he inhaled sharply at the sting.

"I just needed to get out of the house." Her mum handed him a cup of tea before placing another beside her daughter and discreetly left the room. He nodded his thanks and took a mouthful. As it ran down his throat, it briefly sent goosebumps up his arms as it clashed with the cold. He hadn't realised how numb he had really been.

Mikayla looked up at him, concerned etched into tiny lines on her forehead. "Did you have a fight with your parents?"

"Just my mum," he replied, as she pushed out the pieces of gravel which were deeply embedded into the skin. "You should be a nurse," Luke said, as she started to wrap long bandages around his legs, pinning them tight with aluminium claws.

"Ha," Mikayla laughed mirthlessly. "You're the nicest patient I've ever had. Almost done," she said as she started to look at his forearms. He thought back to how it had felt to brush hands with Jamie earlier that day, and regretted, not for the first time, that he didn't have that feeling when Mikayla held his hand. "Your mum must be worried sick though. What time did you leave?" Luke looked up at their kitchen clock and realised it had probably been half an hour. The storm continued to rage outside, the wind whistling through the trees and forcing the branches to knock against the windows. He could barely see across the street.

"I might need to give her a call," he admitted. "Although, she has probably figured out that I'm at yours by now."

His friend raised an eyebrow. "Why is that?"

"Well, other than the fact you only live ten minutes away, my mother has decided that I should probably be deeply in love with you by now. I mean, it has been about twelve years."

Mikayla laughed genuinely this time, and he felt a bit of the tension in his stomach release.

"Yeah, twelve years too long. You're too much like a brother to me, it would be too weird." She smiled at him.

"The feeling is mutual, Mickey. Sometimes, and only sometimes, I think you and Ellie were swapped at birth." She finished wrapping up his arm and leaned back in the old dining room chair she was sitting in.

"Well, while we're on the topic," she looked sheepish for a second, and Luke felt the tension in his stomach return, assuring him that it had only been waiting around the corner. "You might have to find another date to the formal. Jamie asked me this afternoon."

Her words poured freezing water through his veins, as though he were still standing outside in the storm.

He had asked her this afternoon?

They had spent the entire day together and he hadn't even mentioned the formal.

Had he been asking for Luke's permission just by admitting he liked her?

Did Luke even have the *right* to give his permission?

How long had he waited after they had parted ways?

Luke forced a smile, feeling like there was rarely any other kind recently.

"That's… great," he choked out the word.

Mikayla's mum popped her head back in through the kitchen door.

"Can I offer you some dinner, Luke?"

"No thanks, Mrs MacNamara. I think I'll be heading home." Mikayla shot him a look, full of questions, but didn't say anything in front of her mum.

"Let Matthew give you a lift home, then."

"No, thanks, that's okay." As he stood, he felt pain shoot up both his legs, and then his hand, as he grabbed the table to stop from falling back onto his seat. His friend saw him wince and reached out to help him, but he waved her hand away. "Really, don't worry about it." He turned to his friend before she could speak. "That's great news about Jamie, really Mickey. I'll see you on Monday." He hugged her from the side so that he couldn't see her face and limped quickly back out into the drizzle, feeling her gaze from the open door.

The rain let up a little as Luke walked back to his house. He shuffled slowly, trying to avoid his legs bumping against each other or his hands bumping into his sides. He had grazed his palm not badly enough that it was bleeding, but enough that every slight against it was amplified a hundred fold.

As he walked, he thought back to channel flipping a few weeks ago.

Every show had a cute couple in it, who were obviously either meant to be together, were together, or had been at some point. Most of the shows revolved around them, in some form or another - the love triangle, the 'will they, won't they?', the star-crossed lovers. It was like every piece of film, other than some horror movies, was geared towards telling you that this is what you should want. Besides, what is horror for than to play on your worst nightmares? The one you love secretly wants to kill you, or will abandon you in a time of need, or will be used against you by some form of possession. Or even worse, no one loves you. You are alone.

Then some shows had a gay guy in them, but if they weren't the butt of the joke (poorly dressed, overly flamboyant and terrible at sports), they were the wise cracking best friend of some prettier, more popular girl. She was the protagonist, and he was the sidekick, the diversity quota, expendable. If he got too boring, they could always kill him off or have him move away. Or, if he was loved enough by fans, turn out to be straight so that he could end up with the pretty girl. *That's* what we call a happily ever after.

A few shows had a gay couple in them, not usually the main focus but a side plot, and whenever they had been in a relationship, the conflict didn't always seem to come from within the relationship, but because they were together at all. He could imagine the same fights arising, the same uncomfortable conversations and relationships lost because they refused to accept him. Luke didn't even know whether he wanted to date a guy - would he jump at the chance, if Jamie had asked *him* to the formal? Would it be worth coming out to his parents, to the school and Mikayla, battling his own faith?

He paused to lean against a fence, resisting the urge to slump down onto the concrete again.

Not that it was a problem. No one had asked him to the formal, least of all Jamie. Even if he decided to date, there was no one to start a relationship with. He had been relegated to the gay best friend for a while now, he realised, and now that Mikayla had met her love interest, there was no reason for him on the show.

He would never be the main character.

7

Church

He hadn't been able to stop thinking. He had a headache from the constant movement of thoughts, taking off and landing, squirming restlessly in his mind.

If he wasn't thinking about Jamie and Mikayla together, a sting from one of his grazes would remind him of the awful conversation with his mum. He kept thinking of them going to the formal and having to explain why he was sitting at home, by himself. Surely that would be better than going and having to see them together all night?

When he had walked through the door, he had headed silently upstairs for a shower, dripping wet, and then hobbled to the kitchen for a sandwich. Just as he had reached the kitchen, he heard parts of a conversation floating through the partially open door.

"I just don't know what's going on with him these days," his mum was saying. "He was so happy when he walked in, and then I said something and it just set him off."

"Do you remember what it was?" He could picture his dad, leaning against the bench, shoulders hunched as he folded into himself, trying to put together a puzzle he didn't have all the pieces for.

"No!" Her voice was wavering with tears. She was angry, Luke could tell, and maybe just a little scared. "I just asked if he had been out with a girl, just joking around, and he told me that he had been out with Jamie, from dinner last week. I thought that was absolutely lovely, but he just got so angry all of a sudden."

He remembered how quickly it had come on, that anger. He didn't think he could handle any more of what they had to say, so he walked in and silently pulled a plate out of the cupboard.

"Mickey's mum gave us a call, let us know you were on your way," his mum had said softly. He could physically feel the weight of all the things being left unsaid, still hanging in the air. "Dad will go and pick up your bike tomorrow." He pulled two slices of bread out of the bag and quickly swiped some peanut butter on them.

"We were worried about you, son," his father had added. "We had no idea where you were. What happened? What's wrong?" They were looking at the deep grazes on his arms and legs, weeping out in the open after he had carefully unwound the bandages in the bathroom.

"Nothing," he lied, and headed to his room. He had fallen asleep as soon as he had gotten into bed, suddenly no longer hungry. When he had woken up in the morning, the sandwich and plate were gone.

His mum had silently gotten out some Betadine and helped him clean and redress his wounds, but he had spent the day doing anything he could to distract himself, from cleaning his room top to bottom to bingeing three entire seasons of 'The Office'.

Oscar, you're gay. Boom, roasted.

He had considered not going to church that evening, especially knowing that Jamie and his dad would probably be there, but he was rostered on for keys. Besides, anything had to be better than lying around the house while his parents looked at him as if he was a palliative care patient. Or in a mental institution.

***

The pews were almost empty that evening, just the regulars. He sat up the front in his usual spot and didn't comment when his mum slid in next to him, instead of sitting across the aisle with his dad. It wasn't his dad preaching, but their student minister, a well-meaning guy called Simon.

"We have decided not to broadcast tonight's sermon on the livestream," he began.

The church had been posting videos of their sermons for the past few years. There was a group of people who were unable to physically attend church and relied on these videos to participate in the service, talking about them online or during Bible study groups during the week.

"We live in tumultuous times, and there are some messages which are too easily misinterpreted, just asking for trouble," he continued. "However, it's important to still talk about them in a church context. The Bible is pretty clear on a lot of the issues we still debate on in our society today. Tonight we will be looking at Leviticus, chapter 18, as part of our sermon series. This chapter talks about not only the physical consequences but the spiritual penalty for disobeying God's commands." It wasn't church members who he didn't want to listen to his sermon - it was other people, outsiders. What Fuddy had said about trouble came to mind - if that's what they were trying to avoid, the thought of what was to come made Luke uneasy.

"Of course, if you do have any questions about some of the things we do or don't talk about tonight, please feel free to come and talk to one of us on the ministry team." They always did that. They made it so that you had to come and talk to them, which no one was ever brave enough to do.

"All that being said, let's jump into the passage for tonight."

Luke skimmed the passage as it was read out. At the bottom of a long list of sexual sins including incest and adultery, were the words 'do not have sexual relations with a man as one does with a woman; that is detestable.' Just above having sex with an animal.

For his whole life, church had been the one place Luke had felt welcomed and known. The two feelings had gone hand in hand, almost without question. There were people within their church who had known him since he was a little boy. The church lawn had been his backyard, and he had become a part of the furniture. However, since meeting Jamie, something had changed. Suddenly, there was something to hide.

He had been waiting, almost unconsciously, for the moment when he would be forced to reconcile that part of him with the rest of reality, and now it seemed the moment had arrived. As he sat and listened, Luke watched as the gaps in his identity were stretched wide open.

"We live in a society which is looking to identify itself by anything other than its relationship with God. They are seeking to make themselves the rulers of their own lives, and this is the very nature of sin. We can't make room for it. We can't even allow for the *possibility* of it - Jesus teaches us to pray, 'lead us from temptation'. So as a church, we need to avoid opportunities to be defined by our sexuality, our own definitions of right and wrong, this sense of individuality when it means having to choose between God and what is popular. A time is coming for each of us where we have to choose - choose whether we want to be on God's side or not, part of his family or not."

For the month since he met Jamie, he had been having this recurring dream.

There was a beautiful light off in the distance, a golden glow emanating from around a throne, encrusted in jasper and rubies. A shining rainbow encircled the throne, shimmering like a mirage. It was spinning slowly, not as a perfect circle but shifting, like a million tiny birds moving in synchronised formation. In the throne sat a man, his face impossible to see due to the brilliant lights coming from behind him, a dark silhouette atop a body clothed in white linen. The image was amazing and kept drawing him in, but every time Luke tried to get closer, it seemed like the vision got further away. He would push and push against the invisible hands holding him back, until he watched it move further and further into the distance, leaving behind nothing but darkness. Every time he had this dream, he woke up in a cold sweat, panicking as he groped for the switch of his lamp. It was happening more and more frequently, making him afraid to turn off the light at all when he got into bed.

"In our society, it is becoming more acceptable to commit some of the sins on this list – that's who you are, people argue. Do what makes you happy. But God doesn't have a changing perspective of sin. He has created man and woman to be in monogamous relationship with each other – anything else, even allowing yourself to be tempted, is unacceptable. The Lord commands that any of these practices is reason enough to kick someone out of the community, they are that serious."

Maybe he had already known, a still small voice whispered, that he didn't belong.

That they had always been ready to cut him off.

Luke pulled out his earphones and turned on some music.

He had seen Jamie up the back while he was playing music and hadn't made up his mind whether to avoid him or not. In the end, it was Jamie who came up to him.

"Hey, sorry if I kind of ambushed you yesterday," he said, walking over to where Luke was standing near the snack table. "I heard that you hadn't asked Mikayla to the formal yet, but I wanted to check with you first to see if it was okay to ask her." Luke attempted to look nonchalant.

"Yeah, no, it's okay." Jamie looked down and saw the bandages wrapped around Luke's knees beneath the bottom of his shorts.

"What happened there?" The concern was clear on his face, etched into a tiny little line above his eyebrows. Luke didn't know whether to be flattered or embarrassed that he had even noticed, but trying to drag his jeans over his knees had been agony.

"Nothing, I just fell off my bike last night."

"Last night?" Jamie was incredulous. "Wasn't there like, a crazy storm last night?" Luke shrugged again, looking down at the floorboards. He couldn't help but wonder whether Mikayla had told Jamie about last night already and he was just pretending not to know. That's how it would be if they started dating, always left out of the loop.

"I dunno," he took a deep breath, trying to loosen the knot in his chest.

"Hey, I really am sorry," Jamie said, reaching forward to put a hand on Luke's shoulder. He couldn't help but flinch away. "I won't take her if you don't want me to."

He was a good friend, thought Luke, even if that was all he'd ever be.

What was the point of three people being unhappy?

"Don't worry about it, really. She'll be over the moon." He turned away to make a cup of tea, barely registering the hot water flicking out of the shallow paper cup. "What did you think of the sermon?" If Jamie noticed the abrupt change in topic, he pretended not to.

"Ah, I thought it was pretty good," Jamie said, nodding thoughtfully. "I mean, we don't usually talk about that sort of stuff in church, right? That sort of nitty gritty, what does it actually mean to live this out sort of stuff?"

"What do you mean by that?"

"Well, just, I think in today's society, we're kind of getting so that you can't even say what you really think or what the Bible really says without offending someone. I thought it was really brave of Simon to say no, the church is still against same-sex marriage or like, incest and stuff and it's still really important to God."

"So brave that he didn't want anyone else to know."

"You mean with the livestreaming?"

In the end, Luke had seen why they hadn't wanted to broadcast the sermon. It went against almost everything society was saying at the moment. On one hand, he finally had a definitive answer for how the church viewed people like him; on the other, he had never thought it would feel so lonely. Simon had continuously referred to it as 'same sex-attraction' or SSA, which sounded like some sort of disease.

Luke nodded.

"Yeah, but you know, people can get fired these days just for going to a church that says that sort of stuff. I get where he was coming from."

"And he didn't just say getting married, he made it sound like even the thought or feelings were wrong. Man, it felt like he was saying even calling yourself *gay* is wrong." Luke didn't realise he was getting steadily louder. His fingers were curled into tight fists, his fingernails cutting into his palms.

"Yeah, but everyone has to rein it in sometimes. Like, you know, if you're a really angry guy, or struggle with gambling –"

"But those things hurt people, they tear families apart." Luke interrupted. "How is loving someone on the same level?" He searched Jamie's face for some level of understanding, some feeling that he might be at least supportive, but he just looked slightly bewildered. They stood there for what seemed like hours, neither able to read the other's thoughts.

"I'm sorry, Luke," Jamie said eventually. "I'm still new to all this, you know? Still trying to figure it out myself."

"I'm sorry too," Luke said, as he swallowed the bitter dregs at the bottom of his cup.

8
Pride

On Monday at school, Mikayla and Jamie had tried to pretend that everything was normal.

He found ways to get out of sitting with Mikayla and Jamie, volunteering to help out at the library at recess, cleaning up after art and actually listening to the teacher for once and studiously taking notes.

Anything to help him ignore the knot in his belly every time he saw them together.

By the next day at lunch, he'd had enough of pretending.

He headed to the oval to play football, calling out something about practising for their next game.

Technically at school, students weren't supposed to tackle – to get the ball off someone, you were just supposed to touch them, and six touches meant turning the ball over. However, up the back of the oval, there was always a game going. Whenever a teacher was within proximity, someone would yell 'touch!' and the game would transition seamlessly from one code to another, and back again once they yelled 'gone!' Although it was technically breaking the rules, these guys were trying to prepare for the big leagues – these were the rules of proper rugby.

He joined the outskirts of the game, keeping his eye on the ball. One of the guys didn't see that he had joined in and dodged his way. He lunged forward and aimed for their knees, knocking them to the ground. Even after a few days, his knees hitting the ground sent shooting pains up his thighs. It felt good.

He watched as another one of their team scooped the ball up and walked backwards, waiting for the next round, steeling himself for impact. He let them run forward a few metres before pouncing again, feeling his body slice through the air before he knocked into them. The boy went down with a grunt and Jamie reached out a hand to help him back up. He put down the ball and rolled it backwards with a foot, only to be scooped up by Marcus.

"Good afternoon, Lukey boy. We don't usually see you around here." Luke was reminded of the old western films he used to watch with his grandpa. *This town ain't big enough for the two of us.*

He put the ball into the crook of his arm and laced his fingers together, bending them backwards until the knuckles popped.

They both took a few steps backwards. Marcus grinned and spat on the grass to his side. There was no whistle, no signal, but they knew when the game had started again. Marcus lunged forward, a ferocity which hadn't been in the other boys – a malice. Luke dodged to the side and felt like a bullet train had whizzed past him. Shaking his head, he started after Marcus, dodging and weaving his way through the other boys, training his gaze on his target. Soon, everyone else had fallen behind. The goal in sight, Luke put his head down and just charged. There was a pause, a brief gap of nothing, before his head met the centre of Marcus' back and they both went down. He wrapped his arms around the other boy, grabbing his left hand with his right and tightening his muscles like ropes. They hit the ground with a thud, the ball spinning off to the side.

Both groaned and rolled onto their sides. The other boys came over, mostly out of fascination.

"You okay, Marcus?" It was Tricky Taylor. Luke coughed and stood, brushing the dirt off his shorts.

"Yeah, I'm alright," Marcus said, looking up at them, that same old grin still stuck to his face. "I'm sure Luke is too."

His head whipped around. "What's that supposed to mean?"

"No hard feelings, Luke, I'm sure everyone's thought about doing it once in a while." A murmur swelled in the crowd.

"I genuinely have no idea what you're talking about."

"So you didn't mean to cop a feel on the way down?" Everyone within earshot burst out laughing, while Luke's face was lit aflame.

"Get a room, you two!" someone down the line yelled out.

"Buy him dinner first, Luke!"

"What the hell?" he hissed at Marcus, but he knew. The year seven kid.

"I'm just kidding, PK." He rolled back onto the balls of his feet and stood up, stretching out like a taipan. When Marcus got to his feet, Luke shoved him in the chest. Marcus raised both hands in mock surrender. PK, pastor's kid. "I just don't appreciate you getting too friendly, is all."

"I didn't touch you." His voice sounded almost like a snarl.

"Yeah, just keep telling yourself that."

That was the problem, though. It was something he had to tell himself every day – don't play wrestle, don't look at someone wrong, don't make the wrong joke at the wrong time or they'll *know*.

Luke couldn't help but wonder what the other boys on the team were thinking. A few of them had seen what had gone down at lunch and he wasn't sure whether they believed Marcus. There hadn't been any truth in it, but it had struck a nerve. It reminded him of the reception he would get if anyone found out that he actually was attracted to guys. Gay kids weren't welcome on the footy team – they were something to be made fun of in the locker room, the sort of kid who didn't play sports or get picked in P.E. Every pass which didn't quite make it to him felt like a sign that, slowly but surely he was being iced out of the team.

He was already starting to feel as though he was living a double life at church, and now he realised he was living one on the team, too, waiting for someone to whip off his disguise and expose him for what he truly was.

He couldn't help but wonder whether that would be so bad.

A few of the boys went back to playing, but Luke had had enough. He slowly started making his way back to the edge of the field, to sit in the shade until the bell went.

As he passed her, the teacher on duty stopped him, neon yellow vest glowing in the sun.

"I saw that little shove out there, Luke. Keep your hands to yourself."

***

That afternoon, he still wasn't ready to face them, so instead of running to catch up with Mikayla when he saw her, he veered off down a hallway.

The year before, at the tail end of June, flyers had started going up for a club. Printed on violet paper, they were impossible to miss - 'Peer Pride LGBTQI+ Club - have pride in yourself. All welcome.' Luke had seen them a billion times walking down the hallways, but had never considered going to one.

He had some trouble finding the classroom, tucked away near the art faculty, where he had avoided going for the past few years. There were a few people he recognised from class but he was surprised by the amount of people he didn't know. He couldn't have picked most of them out of a line-up.

He grabbed a cookie from next to the door and went to sit up the back, but as the clock ticked over to quarter past three, people slowly started forming a circle. There was no chance to hide.

"Good afternoon everyone," a kid with bright blue hair stood up the front and addressed the group. "Thanks for coming along. I know assessment time is ramping up and we've all got a lot on our mind, but I'm really happy to see that we've got a new person joining us this afternoon." Everyone swung around to look at him. "Would you mind introducing yourself?" No chance to hide at all.

"Hi everyone," Luke said, leaning forward. Was this how people felt at Alcoholics Anonymous? Not just having to introduce themselves in a circle, but a strange mixture of belonging and shame at the same time, just for even being in the same room as this group of people? "I'm just visiting."

"Well hello, Just Visiting," the kid smiled. "My name is Chris and I'll be chairing this evening. It's nice to have you with us. What are your pronouns?"

Luke's mind quickly raced through vague memories of primary school English as he desperately tried to remember what a pronoun was. "He?"

Everyone nodded in unison, as though he had given an acceptable answer. "Mine are they and them," Chris replied. They were tall and thin, their graceful limbs swaying as they walked, like a human willow tree. They wore the school tie and trousers, which was usually reserved for the boys, but there were little butterfly clips in their hair.

As Chris continued with the topics for the meeting, Luke looked around and felt some of the tension leave his shoulders. He was surrounded by people of all sorts and colours. It wasn't just that the group were particularly multicultural, although they were; most people in the group had coloured hair or were wearing a bandana around their wrist. Some of the girls had different coloured piercings or gemstones on their necklaces, some of the guys had painted their nails an assortment of colours and glitters. No one looked the same, and so everyone fitted in.

For about an hour, the group chatted about different areas of life. He heard stories from people's lives not dissimilar to his own, figuring out crushes and hurtful comments, navigating the school halls until they could get to the pride club on a Tuesday or find time to hang out with their friends. They felt like outcasts of society and its establishments, but that enforced independence was a badge of honour. Maybe independence was the wrong word; it wasn't like they had chosen to be separate, but they had *owned* their exclusion, their isolation from the in crowd in a way Luke wasn't sure he ever could.

As open as they were with each other, about half of them hadn't talked to their parents about their sexuality, afraid of the same conversations Luke was, ranging from awkward to dangerous. He realised that most of them didn't have any support network at all outside the group, and he felt lucky for growing up around church and knowing he had adults he thought he could turn to.

At one point, a girl named Alice asked if he was religious. "I mean, I think I remember someone saying your dad was a Christian minister." Everyone turned to look at him.

"Yeah, I'm a…" The word got caught in his throat. "I believe in God."

"Doesn't God have, like, a problem with people like…" She paused, as she decided whether to include him in their group. "People like us?" she finished. There was an awkward silence.

"I don't know," he admitted. That concern had been growing steadily stronger as he had gotten to know Jamie more. "I've been trying to figure that out myself." By this point, everyone was looking at him, and he tried to figure out if it was curiosity, pity or anger, as if their ranks had been infiltrated by an enemy.

"Are you the sort of Christian to picket gay weddings and stuff?" someone behind him yelled out.

"No," he said, staring at the floor.

"Are they the sort of Christians who would picket yours?" Alice asked quietly.

"No," Luke replied. "At least, I don't think so."

When the group broke up for the afternoon, Chris came over and invited him out to get pizza with a few of them, but he knew his parents would be wondering where he was. The time had flown by and even though the sun had started to set earlier with the oncoming spring, the moon was still visible against the pink sky.

For the first time in a long time, he had felt comfortable just being himself, which was tricky as he was just starting to figure out who he was to begin with.

***

That afternoon, on his way home from school, Luke dropped into the corner store.

His hair was an orangey, auburn red which always seemed to grow up and out rather than down. He had been teased for his freckles and hair since he was a kid, his mum always trying to convince him it was something to be proud of, and everyone else was just jealous. That was easy for her to say, with her flowing waves of blonde. His dad had either been shaving his head, bald or a mixture of both for as long as he could remember, keeping his scalp covered with a hat in summer and a beanie in winter, so he had never had to worry. Ellie had gotten their mother's genes, so it was always Luke who stood out, literally like a sore thumb, in family photos.

He pulled on the thin, transparent gloves that had come in the box, and carefully poured one bottle into another, watching the viscous white liquid slowly turn to a grey sludge. He was sick of standing out, and being different - he wanted to control what he looked like, how others saw him, for once.

He squirted the foul-smelling concoction into one gloved hand and ran it through his hair, watching it coat his hair and knowing that there was no turning back now. He put a towel around his shoulders and rubbed his hands through the shorter stubble at the back of his head.

For the next twenty minutes, he paced anxiously backwards and forwards in the bathroom, like a tiger confined to its cell. He thought of what his mother would say, what his friends would think and looked at the gloves in the bathroom sink before shoving them and everything else back into its box. But as he stepped into the shower, the burning hot water running over his shoulders and back, the water around him slowly turning black, he felt his muscles relax, deeply breathing in the steam and the scent of the conditioner. He pushed his fingers through his hair again and again until the slimy feeling was gone and he felt clean.

He admired his handiwork in the mirror.

His fiery red hair had turned the colour of coal.

9

Promotion

His parents hadn't said anything when he headed down for dinner. There had been a controlled pursing of the lips, a slight pause before his mum had resumed setting the table, but it had been Ellie who had broken the silence.

"What on *earth* did you do to your hair?" she asked. He couldn't figure out if it was disgust or respect and then realised, as her older brother, it was probably an even mixture of both. "Congratulations, you've completed your evolution into an emo."

He had just rolled his eyes. There were stains around his hairline and on his hands, where he had accidentally dyed. At first, he had started to scrub in the shower, but realised that he liked the thought that the darkness was spreading.

The next day, people were complimenting him on his new hairstyle, or smiling at him in the hallways. The people from Peer Pride had been waving at him or coming up to say hello in class, and when the time came for Modern History, he saw a flash of blue hair he recognised. Instead of his usual seat in the second row next to Jamie, he went to join his new friend up the back, ignoring his friend's waves.

"Absolutely love the new look," Chris said, with a wild grin. "I'm no stranger to the bottle myself, but black is a bold choice." They ruffled a hand playfully through his hair.

"Thanks," Luke said, feeling himself blush. At least his face wouldn't all be the same colour every time he got embarrassed for a while.

Sitting with Chris was a very different vibe from sitting next to Jamie up the front. He found himself able to concentrate during class, as his friend studiously took notes and copied off the board instead of doodling in the margins like Jamie had. Chris had started their assessment draft and had different coloured highlighters for everything, which they let Luke use. Even the smell was different, more citrus based and fresh. When the bell went for lunch, instead of rushing out, he hung back and kept chatting, only half concentrating as he started following them to their area of the quad.

"Luke!" Mikayla called out to him and he turned around, jolted back to reality. Chris smiled and cocked their head to the side, waiting for Luke.

"I'll catch up with you in a second," he said. How long had he thought he could avoid her?

"Where have you *been* recently, man?" Her voice was high and tense, as though she was straining to hold back all of her emotion. In all of their years of friendship, he had never felt like he had disappointed her before. Until now. "And what have you done to your hair?"

"I just wanted to try something different," he said as casually as he could.

"But your hair was so beautiful." She reached out to touch it, almost as if she couldn't believe her eyes.

"People change, Mikayla," he gently moved her hand away. "I just felt like it wasn't really me."

"Your *hair*? How much more 'you' can it get?"

"Seriously, just leave it." She was the only person that day who hadn't liked it - this was the reaction he had been expecting from his mum. Maybe that was part of the problem. "I'm going to sit with Chris for a little bit, okay? Just give you and Jamie some space to be a couple or whatever."

"Have we done something wrong?" Her voice was so quiet, it was almost a whisper. She looked as though she was on the verge of tears. His heart broke, just a little.

"No," he stepped forward, about to give her a hug, comfort her, and stopped himself. "No, you haven't done anything wrong. I told you," he looked over at Jamie waiting in their usual spot, watching their conversation, "I just need a change."

There were a couple of people in the group who Luke recognised either from Peer Pride or from his classes, but there were a few kids he didn't recognise as well. Once again he was surprised by the diversity and realised that a lot of the kids on his footy team or at his church kind of looked the same. They went around the circle and introduced themselves as he sat down.

"How are you going with your Modern History assessment, Luke?" Chris asked, pulling out their lunch. He was surprised to see it was as boring as his, a ham sandwich. He smiled sheepishly.

"Maybe you should tell me how you're going with yours first."

Chris pulled out their notebook and a few biographies, the pages of which were littered with multi-coloured sticky tabs. They opened up to a page marked with a yellow sticker and showed Luke a photo of an older man with a bushy white beard wrapped in a rainbow scarf.

"This is Gilbert Baker, and he designed the gay flag as you know it today. He was an activist, an artist, a drag queen, and was asked by his friend to draw something which represented the diversity of the LGBTQI+ community. Originally, the colours were all meant to represent something individually, from healing to peace. He's kind of my hero at the moment."

Luke flipped through the images in the book. In every photo, the man was surrounded by colour. There was an image of him wearing a vermilion beret, an emerald green beanie, a cobalt button down shirt under a raspberry red cardigan. He had even worn a rainbow shirt and tie when meeting the American president. The page was saturated with colour.

"So, now that you're sitting with us, can I ask you a question?" Chris asked, a cheeky smile on their lips.

"Go ahead," Luke replied.

"When did you realise you were gay?" Chris asked nonchalantly, leaning back on their hands.

"Chris!" One of the other girls was mortified. "You can't just ask stuff like that!" Luke had never used that description for himself.

"Daisy, don't tell me you're not curious about how the pastor's kid ended up at Pride yesterday. He's sitting with us now, so I'm guessing it wasn't just to like, spy across enemy lines or whatever."

The girl called Daisy looked sheepish and Luke realised that a few people in the group had gone quiet and were pretending not to eavesdrop.

"It's okay, I want to answer." He thought for a second. "I think I've known for a while."

He remembered watching a movie with Ellie when they were kids, one which was still a favourite.

There was a beautiful, blonde princess who had needed saving several times, and sword fights, and adventure, but out of all of the characters, Luke had been most captivated by the Dread Pirate Roberts. Witty, strong and effortlessly handsome, he had realised as Ellie gushed about him, he felt the same way. As his little sister had developed her first crush, so had he.

"I think I've been attracted to guys since I was little, but I haven't really had any real-life crushes, you know?"

"Like, the sort of attraction to one specific person, when you just can't stop thinking about it?" One of the other girls chimed in, who was leaning against the shoulder of Daisy, who Luke assumed was her girlfriend. "That's how I feel about you, babe," she said, smiling goofily at the girl, who gave her a gentle shove and rolled her eyes.

"Shut up, Clarice." She pouted and Daisy relented, pulling her back into the nook of her collarbone.

He thought back over the past few weeks. "Exactly."

Suddenly, a whole group of people knew something about him he had never told anyone else, and he felt okay about it. Better than okay, it felt freeing.

"Do you have a crush at the moment?" Chris asked, leaning forward curiously.

He started pulling bits off his crust and chewing them slowly. "Yeah," he said eventually, looking across the quad at Jamie and Mikayla. Mikayla was no longer looking over at him. "But it's never going to work out," he finished slowly.

"Why?"

"Well, I'm pretty sure he's straight." The way he was looking at Mikayla right now was confirmation enough of that.

"You never know," Clarice said, looking up at him with pity. "People can change their minds."

"Yeah, but you can't wait around forever," a clever looking Asian boy with metallic blue glasses chimed in.

"Let's talk about something else, before the poor boy bursts into tears," Chris said suddenly, clapping their hands together, saving Luke from his train of thought. "What sport do you do on Wednesdays?"

Luke was immediately relieved to have the chance to talk about something he actually knew about.

"I'm the co-captain of this year's footy team, actually," Luke replied, still fiddling with his hands.

"Oh man," the girl Clarice was leaning on rolled her eyes. "For heaven's sake, don't get Chris started on the football team." Luke held up his hands in innocent surrender.

"Why, what's wrong with the football team?"

"Well," one of the boys leaned forward. It was only close up that Luke could see that what Luke had thought was a mole was actually two black studs in his eyebrow. "Christina here -"

"Don't make me fight you, Adrian," Chris growled.

"As I was saying," he said, flashing them a cheeky grin. "*Chrissy* here wasn't even allowed to audition -"

"Try out," someone yelled from behind Luke.

"Because she's a girl and it's only a *boy's* team." He dragged out 'boys' like it was a curse word.

"Oh man," Luke thought over his team, steadily making its way up the ranks. The amount of points they were winning by got smaller every week as they versed harder teams, with more substitutes to swap out tired or injured players. "We could actually really use another player."

"We have seen our fearless leader throw a ball at least a kilometre," Clarice chimed in with serious, wide eyes.

"Well, maybe I could ask the coach, see if he'd be open to at least having you on as a sub."

"I knew we'd like this one, folks," Chris grinned.

That afternoon, as the bell went and people started to head home, Chris ran up to him in the hallway. As Mikayla walked by, she gave Luke a quizzical thumbs up - *coming to the nursing home?* Luke nodded and she kept walking, Jamie magically materialising by her side. It was becoming more and more common to see them together, Luke had noticed, almost as if they were magnetised.

"Hey, I wanted to tell you that on Sunday, a bunch of us are headed to Newtown if you wanna join." Luke thought about Jamie, and his dad, and being rostered on for piano during the evening service.

"That would be great," Luke replied.

That afternoon, he headed to the nursing home by himself, running to join the tail end of students from his school. When he walked in, Mikayla rolled her eyes jokingly and pointed at her watch, but there was something about the smile which didn't quite reach her eyes. He knew that he had been ignoring her for the past few days, but couldn't bring himself to feel anything other than relieved that they hadn't seen much of each other during the week.

On his way towards his usual armchair across from Fuddy, he noticed the old man was reading his Bible, silently mouthing along the words as he went. As Luke sat down, he realised that the words of the Bible were not actually in English, but in lines and squiggles he didn't quite recognise. He sat and waited patiently until the old man was finished. Finally, he looked up and gently placed the book back on the table beside him.

"What language was that?" Luke asked.

"Bulgarian. It's Cyrillic or Slavonic script, also used by Russia and Serbia." Fuddy picked up the chessboard and unfolded it across the coffee table in between them. "I spent some time there as a young man and like to try and keep my brain working by tracing over it."

"Why were you over there? The Cold War?"

"In a way, yes. I went over as a missionary once my time in Vietnam had ended. They were quite desperate for Bibles, especially during the Cold War. I didn't look like much of a threat back in those days - I suppose maybe I still don't," he chuckled to himself. "We quite often take for granted the access we have to God's word in Australia."

Luke thought of the shelf in his father's library which was just Bibles in different translations, from different periods of time. Whenever a new person visited their church, his dad made the same joke - "although I'm usually against stealing, if you are new or visiting and don't have a Bible of your own, please take one." It was the same, he knew, in most churches and Christian organisations.

He began setting up his side of the board.

"So it was illegal?"

"Yes, I suppose it was. That sort of thing didn't matter to us, though. I'm sure you know what it's like to be blinded by the mere importance of something to its consequences." He smiled kindly. "Are you ready to begin?" Luke nodded and Fuddy slowly slid a pawn forward two spaces to begin the game. "I noticed that you didn't walk in with your friends this week." The old man didn't miss a thing.

"I was caught up at school talking to another friend of mine."

"A volunteer here?" He looked around at the other students.

"No, Chris isn't part of the program." Luke slid his own pawn forward.

"A young lady friend, then?" Luke paused as he carefully considered his words. The idea of Chris not having a gender might send the old missionary over the edge.

"Not... exactly. Someone who is trying to figure out who they are."

"Ah," Fuddy said, rubbing his hands together, "aren't we all?" Elmer slid another pawn forward, his crooked and pale fingers shaking slightly as they gripped the tip of the piece. "So is there a romantic interest in your life at the moment? Mikayla perhaps?" He sounded innocent enough, but there was a faint glimmer in his eye.

"Uh, we're not really... each other's type," he replied. He looked down at the board, trying to figure out the strategy Elmer was going with. He felt trapped as he mirrored his friend's action once more, as though he were doing exactly what Elmer wanted.

"Oh really? She does seem quite lovely." The old man advanced his knight, swinging it around to the right.

"She's alright," Luke replied, "just not a Christian." He had a hundred reasons not to date Mikayla lined up, ready for someone like his mother asked. He wondered whether people ever asked Mikayla and, if they did, what she said.

"What sort of church do you go to? Would they have a say in who you decide to date?" Fuddy looked up carefully at Luke as he thought it over.

The first group of people who came to mind were the old ladies who organised morning tea. They seemed gentle and sweet enough to your face, but if you did anything which irked them, even remotely, the whole church would know about it by the next week. He couldn't imagine them finding out he was gay, especially not after the sermon last week. The evening congregation was a bit younger and by proxy, a bit more accepting, but even discussing his love life with *them* would be torture.

"They're alright," he answered finally, advancing his knight by swinging it around to the left. "I do kind of feel like they have a say in what I do with my dating life, though. And I definitely don't think they'd approve of me dating a non-Christian," he added.

"A lot of eyes on you though, I can imagine, especially being the minister's son."

"I guess so."

Just before his grandma had passed away, he had watched his mum grieving at the dining table before going to set up morning tea for everyone before the service ended, turning her emotions off like there was some hidden switch. Now that Jamie was thrown into the mix, it was becoming even more important to master that switch himself.

"So if not Mikayla, is there someone else in your life? A young man, perhaps?" Very gently, almost reticent, the old man knocked over Luke's knight with a tiny pawn. How hadn't he seen that coming? Luke went on the defence and moved his bishop forward two spaces.

"What do you mean by that?" He tried and failed to keep his voice level.

"Well, especially in today's society, it would be presumptuous of me to assume that you are only interested in the other gender, particularly if you're worried about your church finding out." It felt like everything Fuddy knew was now being used against him. There was nothing in his tone to suggest it, but Luke felt as though he were being attacked.

"I'm not gay, Mr Elmer." He almost spat out the word.

"There would be nothing to be ashamed of if you were, Luke." Fuddy advanced his rook. "I mean, I am attracted to men myself." Luke's head whipped up and he studied the old man for signs he was trying to make a bad joke, but only found the usual serene authenticity. He realised he was leaving himself vulnerable and shifted his king to the right, trying to hide it.

"And what makes you think that might be me?" Luke asked, looking around to see if anyone was paying attention to their conversation.

"Something about the way you look at that young man, perhaps?" Luke felt sick. If Fuddy had noticed after seeing them together once, what if someone else had? What if Jamie had? "As I said, there is nothing wrong with those feelings."

"My church certainly thinks there is." He couldn't stop the words from slipping out. "The minister on Sunday said we shouldn't even let ourselves be tempted to do the wrong thing, or we'd be cutting ourselves off from the kingdom of God."

"There is nothing sinful about temptation alone - Jesus himself was tempted. It is what you do with those feelings that matters." His white pawns took another of Luke's pieces, advancing to the furthest row on the board. "I remember what it was like to be your age and almost afraid of how I felt." Luke thought back to his dreams, the feeling he got whenever he was around Mikayla and Jamie recently. Perhaps he really was afraid, or he would have told them by now. He sat, silently staring down at the board, lost as Fuddy turned his piece around.

"In chess," Fuddy continued, "when the pawn moves to its last rank, it gets a promotion. What seems like the least significant little piece on the board becomes the most powerful one - something which once seemed helpless is transformed."

Luke looked at his king, lying helpless next to the pawn. "Check mate."

10
Newtown

That Sunday was cold and pouring rain.

Luke told his family he wasn't feeling well on Friday night, and managed to avoid most of them all of Saturday, pretending to be in bed, eating soup and drinking the cups of tea and honey that his mum brought up for him. On Sunday morning, he wrapped himself in blankets until he heard the front door close, then slipped into his recent uniform of a black hoodie and jeans. It was one of the first times he remembered skipping church and definitely the first time he had lied about why.

He sat on the bus, headphones on, wondering whether he had made the right decision until he reached his stop. There, sitting outside a cafe, was Chris. Clarice and Daisy were there, along with a boy he recognised from Wednesday called Matt and Adrian, who had told him about Chris' endeavour to join the football team. As soon as they saw him, their faces lit up and they started waving. He jumped onto the footpath.

"Let's go on an adventure," Chris said.

As the troupe trawled the streets of Newtown, he tried to take in his surroundings.

Flapping in the wind were rainbow flags, which were also painted on walls and hanging in windows. There was a window filled with teapots, another with pens, another with flowers, another with rubber duckies. The first familiar thing he saw was a mural of Martin Luther King, and it grounded him a bit - he was half an hour from home, not on a foreign planet.

As he walked, he saw people with bright blue mohawks and leather jackets mixed among girls in vintage dresses and high heels. His group blended in, with Clarice in her muted pastels holding the hand of Daisy, who he noticed had slipped in a few more piercings than she was allowed to wear at school. Matt was wearing a tie and oversized business shirt, sleeves rolled up. His black hoodie and hair didn't stand out - if anything, a t-shirt and shorts probably would have.

There were dogs attached to every second person, big and small, fluffy and sleek, old hounds and quick puppies, straining against their leashes. They stopped for some gelato and mixed in among the flavours he knew were a dozen he didn't. He asked for a scoop of neon pink creaming soda.

It was better than anything he had ever tasted.

Around midday, the clouds began to clear and the heat turned the water in the air humid. Sweaty and tired, the group began squabbling over where to have lunch. There were seemingly endless options as they passed frying dumplings, black sticky rice, greasy burgers. They ended up deciding on Italian, the smell of pizza and pasta too much to resist.

As the six of them tried to crowd into the tiny restaurant, they paused at the sound of singing.

Next door was a church, situated a little further back from the street. It looked old and worn, and must have been over a hundred years old. It had stained glass windows, like his church, but there were metal grates covering them, so you couldn't see what the pictures were from the outside.

From the street, you could see that the church was filled to bursting with people. Some had their hands raised, others were swaying side to side, as if the music was dancing with them. Most were singing the melody, but there was a mix of harmonies and just calling out, vocalising, praising God. He had never heard people sing like that before. Although their voices were united, he could hear every single person fitted into their own place. It was an old hymn which he knew well, and he found himself mouthing the words too as everyone read their menus.

"Hey, aren't you supposed to be at church sometime today?" Chris asked, eyes still on the menu.

"I'll try to make the evening service", Luke lied. He had already texted the band leader to let them know he wasn't feeling well.

"That's so cool, that there are different times you can go. When I went with my grandmother at Christmas, she said it was either midnight or nine o'clock in the morning," Adrian rolled his eyes. "I didn't want to admit that I probably would still have been up at midnight anyway, so we went to the proper Christmas Day mass. Most of it was in Latin."

"What's your church like, Luke?" Clarice was looking up absentmindedly as a waitress came to take their orders. Even though her tone had been lighthearted, Luke could feel the atmosphere of the group change, as it had the last time religion had been mentioned.

"It's okay," he said eventually.

For most of his life, church had been about belonging and feeling safe, an extension of his own family as his house was an extension of the hall itself. But now there was a part of him which he could no longer pretend didn't exist. The only thing which was holding him back was the place, the people and the beliefs which had once been so freeing.

"I mean, it's not much different to your average church, although we don't speak much Latin." Adrian winked at him.

"And how do they feel about..." Clarice let her sentence trail off. "Sorry, you don't need to answer if it's too uncomfortable. I know that's a touchy subject for some people." He thought he detected a quick glance in Chris' direction, but their eyes were still on the menu, even though they had ordered.

"Well, I haven't really looked into it much, but not a lot of gay Christians end up in relationships. A lot of them either choose to stay single, or decide not to be Christians any more." He thought back to the sermon last Sunday and added, "The two don't really seem to go together."

"And is that... is that what you want?" Her eyes were wide. "I mean, I know you were talking about how you had a crush the other day, and even though he's straight, is that what you would *want* to choose, to be single? For your faith?"

"I don't know," Luke answered honestly. Jamie could never be interested in him the same way, he knew that, but what if one day someone came along who could?

"Does that mean you're not cool with us dating?" Daisy asked, placing a hand on her girlfriend's shoulder.

"No, no," he hurried to say, shaking his head. "The rules of being a Christian don't apply if you're not a Christian. Like, you're not expected to do other things, like pray or read the Bible."

"Well then I guess I could never be a Christian," she answered firmly.

"It's genuinely not that bad," he said, trying to reassure himself as much as her. "Like, I believe that God has a purpose for me, and that he loves me. That's pretty cool." His words sounded empty and uncertain.

"My dad goes to your church, actually," Chris interjected. They were playing with the paper straw in their drink, bending it backwards and forwards, rendering it useless. Luke realised he had never made the connection between Chris Jones and the middle aged man who attended the

10am service. He had never really chatted to the man, but had seen his name on the service run sheet enough times to be familiar with it.

"I haven't seen you around."

"We don't really get along," Chris said, their voice almost devoid of emotion. "He doesn't really get the whole non-binary thing. I've been staying with my nan for the past few weeks." Luke thought back to the ham sandwich and how he had thought it was so plain, so simple.

There was silence as the waitress returned with their food. Suddenly, no one was really hungry any more.

"I'm just gonna run to the bathroom," Luke said, and walked outside.

He turned his face to the sky as it started to sprinkle and took a deep breath in.

For a second, it had felt like his body was on fire and it was sucking all the oxygen from the atmosphere. He hadn't been able to breathe as he had listened to his new friends voice all of the thoughts he had been having for weeks. A few of them had been hurt so much by something which had been such a big part of his life, and this was a big part of the history between Christians the LGBTQI+ community too.

Was such a big part, present tense? Now the same thing was starting to hurt him.

Wasn't that why he had called in sick?

As he stood under the awning of the restaurant, out of the rain, the service in the little church finished and people started filtering out. Luke could see people wearing pressed suits with collared shirts and ties next to people wearing clothes worn through in patches, others without shoes, men and women, people of all ages and nationalities. The rain didn't seem to bother them, as groups headed off down the street in different directions. Something inside the building caught his eye and, as most people had left, he stepped inside the foyer.

Above him was an enormous mural.

There were angels blowing trumpets, men on snow white horses, flowing water and luscious trees, the sun, stars and moon. It filled the entire ceiling, and Luke almost fell backwards trying to take it all in - the more he looked, the more he saw. The colours were overwhelming.

In the centre of the mural, making a giant, magnificent ring, was a rainbow.

"Can I help you?" A man was standing on the stage, turning off power points and winding up guitar leads. He slowly made his way over to Luke, pausing to stare up at the ceiling as well.

"Oh…" Luke tried to think of a logical reason he would be standing in someone's church, staring at the ceiling. "Ah, do you go to church here?"

"Yep," the man answered cheerfully, offering his hand as he reached Luke. "My name is Malachi." His grip was warm and gentle.

"Is your church accepting of …" He glanced up at the mural again.

"Of the other people who love the rainbow? Yeah, they are." He wound a velcro strap around the lead he was holding and hung it up on a hook on the wall. "That's a big part of the reason I moved to this area, actually. It started with running away from home, but that was a little lonely, so I started looking for a community I could belong to. Along the way, I found Jesus. Are you a believer?"

Before he could answer, Luke heard the door open behind him. Chris popped their head in.

"Hey, we were just wondering where you went." They smiled. "Figured the church was a good place to start."

"Hello there!" Malachi called to them, his voice booming in the empty space. "Come on in." Chris looked down at the floor as if worried they would burst into flames as soon as they stepped inside. "Come on, come on," Malachi started walking over. "We don't bite."

Chris looked like they were going to resist again, so Luke pointed up at the ceiling. Shocked, Chris pushed the door open to get a closer look.

"Wow," was all they could say and the three of them stood, studying the different images spanning from one end of the ceiling to the other. "What is this supposed to be?"

"It's the book of Revelations," Luke answered, and Malachi looked surprised. "It's an image of when Jesus will come back, and all of the different things that are supposed to happen when he does."

"What does the rainbow mean?" Chris asked, looking at the two men.

"Well, it's similar to our society," Malachi answered. "Rainbows are a sign of inclusion and peace, but God was actually the first person to put a rainbow in the sky. In the Bible, rainbows are also a symbol of God's promise of peace. They're a reminder to us that God loves people, and loves second chances."

"I hope so, because I'll probably need a few," Chris said, only half-joking. "I'm so sorry, but our friends are waiting for us next door," they said eventually.

"Of course," Malachi said, laying a warm hand softly on Luke's shoulder. He hadn't realised how cold he was. "Thanks for dropping by, and know that you're always welcome."

As they walked outside, Chris turned to Luke.

"I'm sorry for how the conversation went earlier, Luke. We all are."

"It's okay." He tried to muster a smile.

"No, it's not. You must have been so overwhelmed." They reached over and enveloped him in an embrace and he hugged Chris back. "We've just never really had a Christian friend before! We don't know what we're doing." The two laughed and he felt a little bit of the tightness in his chest unwind.

"If it makes you feel any better, I feel the same way about you guys." As the two headed back into the restaurant, he paused. "Hey Chris? I'm sorry about your dad."

"Thanks." Chris smiled sadly. "I just hope it goes better if you come out to your parents."

"So do I."

The rest of the day passed with no drama.

The more time he spent with his new friends, the more he realised they had in common. Some of them watched the same shows or enjoyed surfing, a few of them had a chat about the upcoming Modern History assignment (and hadn't started either), and he realised that the only thing which had been holding him back from chatting to them earlier had been their appearance. He had subconsciously put them in a different box to himself, for no real reason. Letting Adrian suggest clothes for him to try on or talking to Clarice about movies he should watch was something he could never have pictured doing only a few weeks ago, and yet, as he did so, he found himself having fun.

It was only when he picked up a pair of socks covered in footballs that he thought of Jamie, probably sitting down in the church service right now and wondering where he was.

11

Suspended

"Hey there, long time no see," Jamie said, as he sat in his usual spot in Modern History. "You weren't at church or youth group last week."

"Yeah, I wasn't feeling well."

He had never gotten a reply from the band leader on Sunday, but no one else had sent him a message to see how he was going or where he had been. His dad had been waiting up for him, sitting on the couch with Brick reading the newspaper. When he walked in, long after the last service had ended, all his father had said was, "Looks like you're feeling better."

"You rushed out of the nursing home on Tuesday too," Jamie continued.

"I had somewhere to be." That was a lie. He had headed straight home and curled up in bed, watching old shows with his headphones on.

"Sitting with us at lunch today?" He had been planning to sit with his friends from Peer Pride again. As if reading his mind, Jamie replied to himself. "That's alright. We just," he sighed, and it looked as though he were trying to choose his words carefully. "I just miss seeing you around, is all."

"Yeah, I miss you guys too," Luke mumbled.

"Then why are you avoiding us?" He looked up to see Jamie staring directly at him, searching his face. "Damn it, Luke, if I didn't know any better, I'd say we'd done something to offend you."

"Not everything is about you." The blood rushed to his face, pounding in his ears. "You and Mikayla seem to be doing just fine without me."

"Is that what this is about? The fact that we're dating now?"

"Oh, so you are dating? And when were you going to tell me?"

"When did we have a chance? You run out of every room. You never want to talk. You don't reply to messages."

"Well maybe I don't want to talk now." Tears were stinging the back of his eyes, blurring his vision. Jamie was right, he had been avoiding them. It hurt too much to stay and try to figure things out, even now. He stood up to go.

"We *care* about you, man. I just need you to know that."

I care about you too, thought Luke as he walked away.

Neither of them bothered him for the rest of the day. Even though his locker was right next to Mikayla's, he only caught glimpses of her leaving just before he got there. He sat next to people from the Peer Pride group, or alone in the corner of the room if there was no one else he knew in the class, counting down the seconds until the bell rang and that afternoon, he walked home by himself.

His dad was playing with Brick in the yard.

"Interested in a game of catch?" he asked, the dog sitting and waiting patiently until the game resumed.

"Not really, no. I've got some studying to do."

"How was today?"

"Good."

"What did you learn?"

"Nothing." He turned on his heel and started walking up the stairs.

"What are my tax dollars paying for then?" He mouthed the words along with his dad.

Tuesday afternoon meant sport, which was one of the few times during the week he knew he wasn't going to have to deal with friends, new or old.

When he got to the buses, he put on his headphones and looked up the artists that his friends had been talking about in Newtown. Lil Nas X, Hozier, Elton John and Freddy Mercury. Songs of pain, secret love and longing for something more.

I just gotta get out of this prison cell, someday I'm gonna be free.

The other school was already there, doing stretches by the side of the field. His team filed off the bus and crowded around their teacher, who would be refereeing the match.

"Now remember boys, this one is make or break. We win this, we're in the finals, so keep your head in the game and no funny business."

This was the match they had been building towards since the beginning of the term, but now that it was finally here, Luke barely felt anything.

The boys lined up along their side of the field and waited for the whistle to blow.

"Hey Lukey," said Marcus, coming up alongside him. He kept his eyes straight ahead, focused on the ball, trying to drown out whatever was coming next. "I saw you last week, heading off to Peer Pride. You haven't been sitting with your usual crowd."

"So, what's it to you?" Luke was sick of this guy constantly being on his back. Actually, it seemed like everyone was these days.

Their teacher blew the whistle and the ball flew up into the air.

"Faggot."

Instead of running forward, Luke lunged sideways.

His shoulder slammed into his teammate, both of them landing on the grass. He straddled Marcus to keep him still and swung his fist back, hitting blindly in front of him. He felt his fist connect with bone, crunching under his knuckles. All he could see was red, his blood pounding in his ears making him deaf to the cries of people around him.

He felt someone grab him by the shoulders and yank him backwards.

It must have all happened within a few seconds but it felt like it had taken hours. His blood was coursing through his head, his hand, his ears.

"Bloody hell, Luke, we're on the same team!"

Everyone on the team looked horrified. Luke tried to stand up, but someone else knocked him back off balance, onto the grass. He could see a blur of red around where Marcus' face should have been.

***

The ride back to school had been unbearable.

An ambulance had come to the field to pick up Marcus while the rest of the team had played and Luke had sat on the sidelines. His dad had been called to pick him up, so he had watched as his friends let the ball slip through the ranks time and time again. They had only one sub, and Marcus was probably worth two or three players alone. His dad hadn't spoken a word, hadn't even asked what had happened - presumably he had been briefed on the phone. He was refusing to look at Luke, cradling his fist in his lap. His knuckles were beginning to turn purple.

"Mr Rivers, I'm sorry but this behaviour is unacceptable." The principal was looking over his glasses at his father, who sat at least a head above him. "This school has a zero tolerance for bullying." Luke snorted, despite himself. "Do you mind explaining why that is so funny, Luke?" His tone could have turned water to ice.

"Ask him what he said," he said, leaning back in his chair, the ugly grin still plastered to his face. "Hate bullies? The guy you're looking for is Marcus."

"I have to say," the principal pushed his glasses up his nose to examine Luke, "that seems unlikely considering he is the one in the emergency department right now, and you are the one sitting here without a scratch on you."

"We both know Marcus Petrov is no saint, Oliver, or we wouldn't be sitting here right now." Luke's dad sounded surprisingly authoritative and level. "I'm sure there is an explanation to this, as much as the resolution was not violence."

"Regardless," the principal interrupted. "We cannot allow students to resort to fist fights whenever they have a dispute to settle. Now, taking into consideration that I have just received word the nose is not broken, and that the boys are in their final few months of schooling, I do not think expulsion is necessary. However, there must be consequences." Luke scoffed again and his dad gave him a swift kick in the ankle under the table. "I am recommending suspension until the end of the term and that Luke not be allowed to participate in extracurricular sports, including the football team, until at least next term. He can keep up with his classes online, and email his teachers if he needs help. This should be particularly disappointing considering the other team has forfeited and our school has proceeded to the finals."

"Luke?" His dad turned to him, as if checking whether this plan was okay. As if anything was okay.

"Fine by me," Luke said, grabbing his bag and heading for the door.

***

"No school until the holidays means you're grounded until the holidays, Luke," his dad said when they got into the car. Luke snapped on his seatbelt in silence. His dad went to turn the key in the ignition and paused. "No more sneaking out to meet up with your friends when you're supposed to have the flu, no parties or going to the beach." Luke didn't reply. Finally, his dad broke the silence, sounding exasperated. "What did he say that made you hit him?"

"Doesn't matter."

"Yes, it does matter. You've just been suspended for two weeks. What has gotten into you lately?" His dad started the car and glanced into his rear-view mirror. "That is so unlike you, Luke." It seemed like a lot of people were asking him that these days.

"You have no idea what I am like," Luke muttered under his breath.

"Do not speak back to me, young man. You are in enough trouble as it is." They pulled out of the school's parking lot as the bus with the football team pulled up at the school gates. "Haven't we taught you anything over the years? What happened to turning the other cheek?"

Luke scoffed. "I *have* been turning the other cheek. I have been letting people throw punches my entire life without defending myself and do you know what that has gotten me? It turns out you just keep getting hit, Dad. It never lets up."

"So what? Now you're just the kind of kid now who strikes first? You're going to get down to their level and break some kid's nose because you woke up on the wrong side of the bed? You are better than that, Luke."

"And what if I'm not? What if I'm *exactly* like that Marcus kid, huh?"

"What are you saying?"

"I'm saying that at least no one messes with him. Just for *once* in my life, I wanted someone to feel like you can't just say stuff like that and get away with it, you can't just pick on me because I'm the nice kid, I'm the

Christian kid, I can take it. Damn, you know what? I just can't take it any more." He kicked his foot against the glovebox and pushed himself back into the seat.

"Stuff like what?" His father was so quiet he almost hadn't heard him.

"You have no idea what he says about other kids, dad."

"What did he say to *you*, Luke?" He thought back over that one word that had tipped him over the edge and realised it hadn't just been one word. Weeks, maybe years, of pent-up frustration had been let out on that field.

Being different was always the punchline.

Sometimes it was something stupid you had said, mispronounced a word, something stuck in your teeth. Something you had done. Something you could change.

But sometimes it was something you couldn't.

Race, gender, sexuality, culture, having an unusual name - all of the things that make you who you are. He had never been the punchline, and had always let it slide, waiting for someone else to stand up for the kid who was. Now he knew how it felt.

His dad continued on as if he could read his mind. "I know what that feels like, that you've reached your limit, and I get it, it's frustrating. But if you let yourself give in to that feeling, you'll realise soon that it's insatiable. You'll be a ravenous man turning up to an all-you-can-eat buffet, and by the time you start to feel sick, you'll already have eaten too much. That's the way anger works, Luke."

Maybe it would have consequences in the end, giving in to his anger.

But right now, it just felt good.

12
Party

The next day came and went with no comment. He watched the clock as it passed three, thinking of his new friends at Peer Pride and wondering if they had noticed he wasn't around. He had gotten one message from Chris – "I bet that kid got what was coming to him" – and wondered whether they had been unfortunate to be on the receiving end of his comments before.

There was silence around the dinner table for the most part, everyone chewing on overcooked steak, lost in their thoughts. Even Ellie was mostly silent as they ate, looking at the three other members of her family as if they were aliens.

After dinner she walked into his room, without knocking, again.

"Hey, is it true you punched Marcus Petrov?"

"Yes," Luke had replied, stunned as always by his sister's abruptness.

"Did he deserve it?" she asked, staring at him intently. He hesitated before answering, but once the answer came out of his mouth, he was certain of it.

"I'm sure no one deserves to get punched in the face, but I don't regret it." She pursed her glossy lips and tilted her head to the side, pulling her blonde ponytail through her fingers.

"Do you remember what he did to Angela?" she asked eventually. Luke pictured the little girl, swinging around as Marcus pinned her arms behind her back and spun around. He remembered her crying out for help as the other kids looked on in shock.

"Yeah."

His sister had just nodded and walked out.

By the next day, everyone seemed to know what had happened. Luke received a few panicked messages from Mikayla, and just one from Jamie - "hope ur ok." He hadn't responded to any of them and had received only one more - "are you coming to the party on Saturday?"

When she had got home from school, he asked Ellie whether she wanted to play chess and was surprised when she had said she would give it a go if he went easy on her. He figured that she was just feeling sorry for him, sitting by himself at home all day. They had played for half an hour, as he pictured his friends heading to the nursing home without him and Fuddy waiting in his armchair by the window.

Then, when Friday came around, as the hands passed seven, he watched from his window as everyone gathered in the church hall next door and tried to think of anything other than Jamie. The week before he had purposely missed it but now, he found that he would have given anything to be able to join his friends.

For the past week, he had been so busy trying to distance himself from his old life. Now, a week of it had gone by without him and he realised how far removed he had become. If he thought about it for too long, it hurt, so he tried as much as he could to play games and watch tv until he wasn't thinking at all.

On Saturday morning, out grocery shopping with his mum, he heard his name called out behind him and turned to see the familiar multicoloured mop of hair bobbing towards him down the aisle. It now had flecks of green and orange in it. His mother had managed to contain her surprise after a few seconds and happily greeted Chris, who was shopping with their grandmother. After exchanging pleasantries, both carers wandered off to find the specials of the week and leave their teenagers to chat for a few minutes.

"You'll never believe what happened after you got suspended." Chris grabbed Luke by the shoulders, beaming with excitement. "I tried out for the football team!" They squealed and Luke pulled them forwards into a tight hug.

"Congrats! How did that happen?"

"Well, they just announced on Thursday at roll call that they would be holding impromptu trials at lunch time, and *anyone was welcome.* So, I just thought I'd take them at their word and turn up, and I absolutely smashed everyone else. Besides, they were looking for two people because, you know, they had to replace Marcus as well." Chris gasped at the sight of the blood rushing to Luke's face. "Oh my gosh, no, no, he's fine, I heard that you didn't even break anything. He's just going to have to wait for the swelling to go down a little, and he already had such a big head to begin with." The two laughed and Luke hugged Chris again.

"I know how much you wanted this. Although," he added, "I swear that didn't have anything to do with why I hit him. You didn't, I mean."

"Yeah, about that," Chris looked unusually self-conscious. "I heard one of the guys on the team talking about what happened just before you, you know. You don't have to talk about it if you don't want, but just so you know, we've got your back. Not just me either, but the whole team."

It felt good to know his mates had his back but if Chris had heard, did that mean Mikayla and Jamie had too?

"So, finals next week?"

"Monday as always. My gran is coming, and she invited my dad, but I don't know if he'll be keen."

"I'll try and be there, if I can manage a prison break." Chris laughed.

"I look forward to it."

"Who was that?" his mum asked, when he found her again.

"That was one of my new friends from school," Luke answered, a tinge of pride mixed with the doubt in his voice. "Their name is Chris."

"Their? Is Chris a boy or a girl?" his mum asked, about as subtle as a bull in a china shop.

"Neither, just figuring it out at the moment."

"Ah, you mean asexual? Or is being both bisexual?" Luke smiled at his mother's attempt to use the lingo.

"I mean neither. It's not really a sexuality thing, like who you're attracted to. It's more of a gender thing, like whether you're a boy or a girl. If you don't fit into either of those two categories, then you're non-binary and if you kind of go between them, gender-fluid."

"Right," his mum said, getting a similar tiny little crease in her forehead to the one he got when trying to understand maths homework. "So I guess it's just easier to call them, 'they', then," she said. "Unless, of course," she paused and Luke waited for something accidentally offensive. "Unless that's just bad grammar," she finished. He put his arm around her waist and squeezed. She wrapped her arm around his waist and they walked lopsidedly down the aisle, like two kids in a three-legged race.

***

Party

The next week of school passed by Luke with nothing to mark the passing of time but the LED alarm clock on his bedside table. He was keeping his curtains closed and the music loud in an attempt to forget that outside, everything was going on without him and moving just fine. He was cocooned in his own little world inside his bedroom, with nothing but the occasional meal with his family and toilet break to remind him that he was even still alive.

He had been trying to solve the problem of the party since he had gotten Mikayla's text the week before, but then, in the way that problems seem to solve themselves when you're least sure you want them to, his parents reminded him that Ellie had a dance recital on the 22nd and the three of them would be out. As a condition of being grounded, it was either coming with them or staying at home by himself, so he pretended to choose the latter and when they left, was sitting innocently on the couch wearing an old hoodie and sweatpants.

By the time the car was in the driveway, he was changing into jeans.

Stacey's house was only a few streets from his, so he decided to walk.

His bike hadn't been repaired since he had crashed it a few weeks earlier, and his knees were still a bit stiff anyway, as though he were an old man with arthritis.

The night sky was clear above him, still hanging on to the remnants of the summer light, and it was warm out. As he walked, he kicked a pebble and thought back to walking home with Mikayla.

A few weeks ago, the party seemed like the most exciting thing which could have happened. He remembered how excited she had been even to be invited and talking over what the three of them would wear, but now, it had been days since he had even spoken to his old friends and he wasn't sure he was ready to face everyone wanting to know what had happened with Marcus.

Or people not even caring enough to ask.

No one from youth or church had checked in yet and it had been over a week.

A wave of loneliness swept over him as he turned the corner onto Stacey's street. Despite how awesome his new friends were, he had to admit that spending a week away from school had made him realised he missed his old ones. The people from *Peer Pride* wanted to talk about gender, sexuality, and relationships, which he still didn't have much experience around, or things he didn't have much interest in. He missed being able to have dumb conversations about the newest tv shows without having to do a critical analysis - he often found himself lost in conversation and had only recently learned what the Bechdel test was. The one area of his expertise they were happy to talk about was church, and he was sick of having to defend his faith, especially when he wasn't sure whether he wanted to.

As he reached Stacey's door, he took a deep breath. Maybe this was exactly what he needed.

The room was crowded with teenagers, the smell of sweat and pheromones seeping through every gland and permeating the air. Makeup, which had taken at least an hour to put on, was slowly running down faces in the summer heat, or smudging onto clothes as they bumped up against each other. When they stood up from chairs, they left a moist imprint behind. He felt completely invisible, leaning against the wall.

And then he saw Jamie.

He was wearing a mint-green shirt which looked as though it had been washed a few too many times. The sleeves were rolled up so that you could see his tanned arms, the smooth curve of biceps barely showing. He looked up and smiled, that smile which made Luke's heart want to stop, and skip a beat, and speed up, all at the same time.

"Hey mate, how are you?" Jamie said, walking over to lean beside him. "I don't know if you got my texts, but I heard about the suspension." Luke was grateful that Jamie hadn't sounded accusatory, even though the messages had probably shown that they'd been read.

"Sorry, I got a new number."

"Really?"

"Nope." There was an awkward silence and then, unexpectedly, Jamie burst into laughter. After a few seconds, Luke couldn't help but join in. It felt good to laugh. "I'm so sorry, I have no idea why I said that."

"You are genuinely an awful liar," Jamie said, punching him playfully on the shoulder.

"Noted." Still smiling, Jamie wrapped an arm around his shoulders and gave him a hug. "I really am sorry." Luke tried to fit a dozen apologies into the one word, leaning into the crook of his arm.

"I know."

"I can't believe you're even talking to me, to be honest. I mean, not just for the past week but even the bit before that."

"Mate, I don't know what's going on with you, but I can't believe it's simply that you're just a jerk. So, whatever it is more than that, I'll be here when you're ready to talk about it."

"I hate to break it to you, but I think I might just be a jerk."

"Well, thankfully, that makes you just like the rest of us. Besides, I don't need to punish you."

"Why's that?"

"Because here comes Mikayla."

His old friend was wobbling over, her feet squeezed into bright red heels. She was wearing a sparkly top which Luke soon realised was supposed to serve as a dress as well. It looked silver at first, but shifted colours as she turned in the light, making her look like a disco ball. She had stuck on fake nails and her eyelashes looked suspiciously long. She blended in with the other girls at the party almost seamlessly, but Luke was uncomfortable with how different she looked to her usual self.

She was smiling at Jamie when she saw who was standing next to him and paused just before she reached them.

"Hey Mikayla—"

"Anybody want a drink?" She turned on her heel and walked away.

Someone had brought a few six packs of beer, and although the side of the box said 'lite', the misspelling made it feel like maybe it still had gravity to it. Mikayla pulled a cold one out of the sink, which was filled with ice, and handed it to Jamie, popping off the cap awkwardly with a bottle opener.

"Cheers," she said, raising her drink to the two boys. She winced as she swallowed.

"Cheers, big ears." Jamie took a swig with less of a visceral reaction, so Luke grabbed one for himself and raised the dark brown bottle to his lips. He almost gagged as the grassy, earthy taste filled his mouth. It was almost bitter and burned as it went down his throat. He took another mouthful, purposefully holding his breath so he didn't taste it, and felt his shoulders relax.

He turned to Mikayla to try and apologise again, but before he had a chance a group of teenagers began gathering in a circle on the floor and Stacey Williams was grabbing him by the hand and pulling him in.

"Luke! I'm so glad you made it – you weren't at school this week, so I had no idea what was going on with you." She was wearing a bright orange lipstick and had added some to her cheeks as blush, bringing out the rich undertone of her skin. "Time for spin the bottle!" She dragged him to the edge of the circle and pulled him gently to the floor before walking across to sit directly opposite. She looked graceful and strong, and an image of a tiger rose, unbidden, to Luke's mind. Beautiful but worth being on your guard.

Mikayla grabbed Jamie by the hand and pulled him towards them, instructing her to sit directly across from him as someone placed a bottle in the middle.

They were seated boy, girl, boy, girl, just like they were back in kindergarten.

The bottle was spun.

The first time it stopped, it landed on a couple who had been dating for a few months at school. Everyone knew they had been going out, so it wasn't as awkward when they started sucking face in the middle of the circle and practically had to be pulled apart. Then it landed on two kids who didn't really know each other - the girl just gave him a peck on the cheek. Luke stood up to get another beer from the sink. He found himself less opposed to the taste the more he drank.

Then it landed askew, joining Mikayla and the boy two over from Jamie.

There were a few more turns, and a spectrum of kisses from passionate to pecks.

And then, by some twist of fate, the neck of the bottle landed on Luke. It had spun wildly out of control, almost threatening to leave the circle. He looked up and his eyes met Jamie's. An insane urge to just get into the middle and kiss him overwhelmed him – wasn't that what the game was all about?

Stacey jumped into the middle instead, pouncing into vision.

"I wouldn't mind taking Jamie's place?" Stacey said, applying a layer of pink lip balm and giving him that big, sly grin. He rocked forward onto his knees as she came over on all fours, sat back on her heels and put her hands on his face.

They were cool on his cheeks, and she kissed him.

It was wet, and soft, and sweet.

And he felt nothing at all.

He stood and rushed out of the room.

***

Mikayla found him sitting on the kitchen floor after the game had ended, staring out at the party still raging in the living room. Everyone was lounging around in the living room or hiding in dark corners, but somehow, they had all partnered up for the night. Now even Stacey was curling up next to a boy from the debating team.

"We were wondering where you had gotten to," she said, pulling herself up onto the kitchen bench carefully with her knees to the side so as not to flash him. "Are you okay?"

"Do you really want to know?" he asked, looking up at her.

"Sure I do." She seemed genuine enough, even though he remembered how angry she had been with him, only an hour before.

"I still can't believe that just happened," he said.

"What happened?"

"I just had my first real kiss."

"And it didn't quite go the way you imagined?"

"You could say that." He tipped his bottle upside down to try and get at the last few drops. He was already starting to lose track of how many he had finished off. "I mean, I didn't think there would be fireworks, or angels singing or anything. I just wanted it to be special, with someone I really cared about, you know? And I just don't have anyone like that."

"Well, not at the moment, but you will. I know Stacey definitely has a crush on you." Luke pointed silently to where she was now making out with the boy from the debating team, legs curled around him. Mikayla sighed and slid onto the floor beside him. "Okay, so maybe not Stacey, but you'll find your someone." The words, just variations on ones he had heard so many times before, dug their old familiar claws into his chest.

"How are things going with you and Jamie?"

"Do you really want to know?" she asked with a wry smile. He was hurt for a moment, and then remembered how he had been acting for the past two weeks.

"Yes, I genuinely do."

"Things are going well. I really like him, and I think he really likes me. We've been talking about things for the formal, and gone out to the movies and stuff a few times. I met his dad during the week, more by accident than on purpose, but now we're talking about him coming over for dinner to meet my parents."

"Wow, it sounds like things are moving quickly," he said, looking down at his feet.

"How about you, do you have a crush?" He almost laughed at the irony of the question.

"Not on anyone things could work out with."

"Is that why you've been avoiding us?" she asked. "Because it's awkward now that we're going out? If this is about the formal, I can tell Jamie that I asked you first. I'm sorry that I dropped you like that, Luke, if I've hurt your feelings."

"I'm not talking about you, Mickey." His friend's eyes searched his in confusion, and then started to widen as she realised what he was trying to tell her, maybe what he had been trying to say for years. "I'm gay."

He had spent years worrying what this moment would feel like, how she would react, and now that it had finally arrived, he realised how much he had built it up in his head. Out loud, those two words sounded so small, so insignificant.

"Why didn't you say anything?" she was staring down at her hands, picking at her nail polish. It was also bright red.

"Because my first real crush is Jamie."

For a moment, time seemed to slow almost to a halt. Mikayla may have gasped – he wasn't looking up at her at the time. He heard a bottle dropped to the floor and smash. When he looked up, Jamie was standing in the doorway, a look of panic mingled with something else - disgust? Anger? Disappointment? - etched on his face. Suddenly, he turned and ran for the door.

"Jamie!" Mikayla grabbed the benchtop and pulled herself to her feet. She turned back to look at Luke, fumbling for something to say, and ran off to follow him, leaving Luke by himself.

***

He took his time walking home.

He had rushed out of the party and just started running, but when he was far enough that he was sure no one was following him, he collapsed, legs burning, on the side of the footpath. Who would be following him anyway? It's not like anyone else at the party cared that he was there.

When his breathing didn't slow, he realised he was hyperventilating - the thought occurred to him like an annoying pop up on a website he just wanted to close. He could feel his chest rising and falling arrhythmically, on the verge of a panic attack.

How could he have been so stupid? Why had he let his guard down?

He tried to take a deep breath, his breath hitched, and he tried again, lying back against someone's low brick fence and looking up at the moon and stars. As he watched, a large, dark cloud obscured the moon and he was enveloped in darkness, the branches of the trees blocking nearby streetlamps. He could hear the crickets and cicadas hidden around him, the cool, spongy grass under his fingers. He tried a technique he had learned at school, focusing on what he could see, hear, smell, touch and taste, trying to ground himself in reality rather than get swept up in the zillion thoughts bouncing around his head.

That was why he hadn't spoken to her.

It wasn't just that he was gay - he was sure she would be understanding of that, supportive, even. It was all of the repercussions that was always going to have. Their friendship was changed forever, and the way she saw him, especially now that Jamie was in the picture. A part of him had known since the start of the year that telling her about his feelings for Jamie would force her to choose, to protect her relationship with either him or start a new one.

Maybe a part of him had known she would choose Jamie.

Luke stood up slowly and continued his walk home.

He had known that if he allowed himself to get too close to Jamie, it would only hurt more when he eventually lost him. Mikayla had been his best friend and even she hadn't stuck around. What did that leave him with?

When he shoved the front gate open, however, he didn't turn left, to his front door, but right.

He stepped inside the church hall, empty like a gutted animal, the orderly rows of wooden pews its ribs. His footsteps echoed off the dark brick walls like prayers, but no one could hear them except him. He walked to the altar, carpeted in blood red, and stood, staring up at the image of Jesus seared into the stained-glass window. Even at this time of evening, the moonlight spilled into the church, illuminating the colours of the scene - Jesus, ascending to his heavenly throne as heaven split open, his mother and disciples below looking up, longing to be taken too. The image was cut into a million fractals by blackened copper, lines which Luke had traced as a little boy, bored of waiting for the sermon to end.

"What do you want from me?" he asked the window, his voice too loud for the silence.

Jesus looked down serenely on his worshippers who had gathered at the cross.

There were clean black circles in his feet and hands, symbolic of where the nails had been. Crucifixion, the root of the word excruciating. A type of torture reserved for only the vilest of criminals, given to the man who said he was God. He would have been bloodstained and beaten; his wounds wouldn't have looked like that. Luke looked down at his own hands, scabbed over from falling off his bike. This was a man who was supposed to understand suffering. This was a God who was supposed to know how he felt. But instead, all Luke could see was a pretty picture, mounted quietly in a church, looking down on its worshippers.

He walked up to the altar, past the wooden beams which marked where laymen were supposed to stop, up to the bronze cross sitting on a table against the far wall. Up close, it was pock marked with verdigris from years of disregard, a useless symbol for people too far to see its imperfections. He picked it up - it was heavy - and stepped back until he could see the window again.

"Answer me!" he yelled into nothingness, rage filling his chest and reverberating through his body.

He had lost everything. He was alone.

He raised the statue, picturing the shattered colour raining down on him, the sacrilege he would be committing.

The emptiness enveloped him, and he fell to his knees.

"Answer me," he begged, placing the cross on the carpet in front of him with two hands.

But all he could hear was silence.

13

Cliffs

There was nothing except the wind and the waves below. Summer had officially gone and past, the sun hidden behind layers of mottled grey clouds, and not many people were out on the footpath. Luke had been sitting on the same bench for almost an hour.

His dad had been asleep on the couch, his glasses still on, trying to wait up for him. He figured there would be a tongue-lashing whenever they met next, so that morning, he had gotten up just before sunrise.

He had started at his desk, pen in hand, lined paper in front of him and blanked.

Balled up pieces of paper were scattered all around him, looking like a ring of snowflakes. They all said the same thought, a hundred different ways. Something along the lines of, *I just can't any more.*

He couldn't even figure out what he couldn't do. He just couldn't keep going. There was something wrong.

He had been wrong, wrong, wrong, every time.

Running out on his mum and trashing his bike had been wrong, hitting Marcus had been wrong, going to the party had been wrong.

Maybe telling Mikayla had been wrong. Maybe liking boys was wrong. Maybe trying to be himself was wrong.

Maybe he was just *built* wrong.

Even addressing the note had been hard - he didn't want to write something which made it seem like he blamed them at all, but he also needed to leave an explanation. The whole thing seemed too complicated. He bit the inside of his cheek; he wasn't even strong enough to write this, when it actually mattered.

In the end, he had written two lines.

> *I'm sorry.*
> *I love you.*

He had scrawled his name at the bottom and folded it up into an envelope, leaving it on his desk, and just started walking. Down to the beach, along the footpath, back up the hill to the cliffs.

So, he had been sitting there, staring out at the horizon, tracking the movement of ships and occasionally looking over the edge at the rocks below. He didn't know anything about tides, where he would wash up. He could see the part of the beach he had tossed the ball with Jamie the other day. Back then, the ocean had felt glorious over his skin - today, it smelled like tears.

Should he say a prayer now? That's the sort of thing his dad would do. But what would he pray for?

A few years ago, someone had brought wrist bands to youth group with the acronym W.W.J.D. embroidered on them - what would Jesus do? Apparently, he had heard years later, those bracelets were the most commonly stolen item from Christian bookstores, something Jesus would definitely *not* do. But he had found himself asking himself that question over the years. When given the chance, Jesus had not jumped from a great height onto rocks below, as tempting as it had been. Satan had told him that, if God were really powerful enough, he would send angels to protect him from the rocks below. Years later, Jesus would be tempted to take the easy way out again.

"Father, take this cup from me," he whispered under his breath.

He could not find the strength to utter the next words.

But not my will but yours be done.

He glanced down at his watch; right about now, his father would be finishing the sermon and the band would silently be moving towards the stage as he prayed. He hadn't heard from his church friends in weeks, since he had stopped volunteering to be part of the band. Ellie had occasionally mentioned someone had asked after him at youth group, but for the most part it had been radio silence. As much as it hurt to be forgotten, he realised with a pang that he missed it all a bit.

Down on the beach, the beach was starting to come to life.

Surfers sat atop their boards, bobbing up and down, waiting for the perfect wave. The red and yellow flags flapped in the wind, lifeguards sat atop their towers with binoculars. Soon, people from church would be heading down to grab some lunch.

He wondered absentmindedly whether Jamie and his dad would be among them, or whether they would go to the evening service again. He thought about his family, coming home and finding him gone again.

He wondered how they would feel if he never came back.

His heart broke as he thought of theirs breaking.

It was cold, sitting on the bench, and lonely.

After church, his family would sit down for lunch at the same table they had hosted Jamie and his dad. Sometimes Luke's mum would bring out a nice cake and they would have strong cups of black tea, or he would take Brick for a walk down to the park with Ellie and they would throw the ball for him. He thought of Fuddy, marked by years of sorrow but also times of joy, and he thought of the little girl who had once lent him a pen on his first day of school.

As he looked over the edge and contemplated the drop, there was no urge to jump. The deep sadness which had been welling deep within him for weeks was still there, the confusion about what to do next and how he would ever recover from all that had happened. However, the good was still there too, weaving its way in and out of the bad.

Sitting atop the cliffs, Luke realised that all he really wanted was to go home.

***

When he stepped through the front door, the house was silent.

Luke thought perhaps his family was out having lunch and headed to his bedroom to retrieve his note before anyone saw it. When he pushed open the door, his dad was sitting on his bed.

Paper was still littered everywhere, but the letter was no longer on the desk. As his mind desperately attempted to come up with some explanation, his father crossed the room and folded him into an embrace.

"Luke." The name sounded like an exhalation of a breath held for too long.

He was overwhelmed by the scent of the cologne he saved for Sundays washing over him. He had gotten his dad that cologne for Father's Day. As his father stepped back, still holding him by the shoulders, Luke looked his father in the eye, watched the tears trace the path of his smile lines down his weathered cheeks, and saw himself reflected in his dad's glasses the way his dad saw him. Small, his black hair tugged this way and that by the wind, a million directions at once, his cheeks hollowed out and his eyes gaunt. He looked tired. "Where have you been?" his dad whispered, his voice raw with emotion.

"I walked down to the beach," Luke replied, trying to pack paragraphs into his words. His dad took another step back and let himself fall onto the bed, dragging his son towards him as he sat. Luke sat beside him and his dad put a warm hand over his own. The blue veins stood out, in stark contrast to the papery thin skin covering them, dotted here and there with freckles, moles and scars. A faded gold wedding band sat on his finger, etched with years of wear. He could feel his dad's pulse in his fingertips, still racing.

"Ellie found your note," his father said, picking it up from the bed-side table. Luke could picture her walking into his room without knocking again, under some false pretence. "She came to find me." He noted for the first time that his father was still wearing his tie, loosened at the collar. He was also wearing his dress shoes, as though he had run into the house in a hurry.

"I'm sorry, dad," Luke whispered, resting his head on his father's shoulder. His dad ruffled a hand through his darkened hair.

"No, no, don't be. We're your parents, we're meant to worry about you." His dad ran a hand through his son's hair. "We love you, Luke, your mother and I. So, so much. And so does Ellie, in her own way."

"I know. I love you too."

"Whatever is going on, you know we're here for you, right?" Luke had pictured his dad saying those words so many times, unable to believe that they could be true. However, sitting beside him, breathing in his scent and listening to his deep voice, there was no doubt in his words.

"Even if I've killed someone?" He felt his dad laugh.

"I'm sure we could figure it out together."

"Even if I'm gay?" His dad pulled him closer.

"We will figure it out together."

He didn't know how long they just sat there, side by side on the bed, lost in the silence.

After a while, his mum knocked on the door and popped her head around the frame, letting in a slinky Brick who came to sit at his feet. She raised an eyebrow and chuckled.

"Look at the state of this room!" Luke kicked at one of the balls of paper and Brick pounced on it, sending a dozen other balls flying and setting him off again as he tried to chase all of them at once. She bent down to pick up one of the pieces of paper and, without looking inside it, threw it into the recycling bin beside his desk. In his Sunday best, his father got down onto both knees and scooped up a bundle of papers into the crook of his arm. Luke got down onto the floor as well, grabbing his letter and a few other balls of paper, and together the two of them cleaned up the litter.

14

Reconciliation

Church that evening had more people than usual.

The sun was still setting after the service had started, so it was filtering through the stained glass, splattering colour over the wooden pews and floorboards. Up the front, the brass cross stood once more on the altar. It looked as though someone had recently given it a polish. Luke's dad sat next to him up the back, rather than in his customary seat in the front row. He was surprised at how deep his voice sounded when they sang, booming through the echoey hall. Even with only a few dozen people in the room, their two voices mingled together in beautiful harmony.

Whatever my lot, thou has taught me to say it is well, it is well with my soul.

His dad didn't leave his side until he got up to preach the sermon.

"For the past few weeks, we have been looking through the book of Leviticus. It has not always been an easy ride and, in the moments we have stumbled as a preaching team, I ask that you forgive us." Luke had never heard his dad apologise from the pulpit before, and thought of Simon's sermon. What would have happened if he had been brave enough to talk to him afterwards, let him know how it made him feel?

"Keep your Bibles open tonight and, as my kids' teachers used to say, your listening ears on as we finish up Leviticus 19." Luke grabbed a worn, dog-eared bible from the pew in front of him and turned to the passage.

"When the Israelites are first given the law by God, through Moses, they have 10 rules, the Ten Commandments. By the time we finish the book of Leviticus, they will have over 600. They are living lives so rigidly dictated by rules; they are rightfully concerned about stepping out of favour with God. So, it should come as a shock to us that when Jesus came to earth a few thousand years later, it is the people who are following the rules best that he rebukes. He would rather hang out with prostitutes, tax collectors and the sick than the people who have made it their life's mission to follow the law."

Even though he was preaching to the whole congregation, Luke felt like his dad was just chatting to him one on one.

"In the gospel that my son is named after, Jesus tells a story about a young man who leaves home and gets a little lost. He had decided to try and do things his own way. He is a rule-breaker, a rebel, and a screw up. But when it all goes wrong, he thinks his actions have irreparably ruined his relationship with his father. In the story is also an older brother, who has been working the fields. He is a hard worker, and the perfect son. He keeps all of the rules and doesn't doubt that he is his father's favourite.

"Some of us here are that older brother. We have been Christians our whole lives and never done anything wrong. It can be easy to get caught up in the routine of it and become over-familiar with our church, our Sunday routines, and assume that God really likes us. But some of us here are younger brothers. We have gone our own way and gotten a little lost. Maybe you're not sure what God thinks of you right now. The radical nature of the gospel is that *both* are welcomed back home.

"Now, there are certainly rules in the Bible that we need to follow. We need to allow the Spirit to change our hearts, align them with God's will and Leviticus is full of practical ways to do that, lots of *how.* But if you look a little closer, it also gives us the *why.*

"Verse 18 says love your neighbour as yourself. I am the LORD. Verse 32, show respect for the elderly and revere your God. I am the LORD. Verse 34, the foreigner residing among you must be treated as your native-born. Love them as yourselves for you were foreigners. I am the LORD.

"We love people because we love God. This is so important to understand that when Jesus is asked thousands of years later what the two most important commandments are, he will quote Leviticus. 'Love the Lord your God with all your soul, mind and strength and love your neighbour as yourself.' Following the rules is not just about following the rules, which is good news for those of us who are really struggling to.

"We love the prodigal son, because God does. We love the outcast, the reject, the rebel, the screw up, because God does. We welcome the lost, the lonely, those we disagree with, because God does. And we allow God to fix them, to change them to be more like his son. That is something he can do, no matter what they are struggling with."

His dad picked up his sermon outline and tucked it behind his bible, looking up at everyone.

"For those who are struggling tonight, feeling inadequate or lost, starting with the law and wallowing in your shame is not going to get you anywhere. Trying to be perfect is putting the cart before the horse - this church is a hospital for sinners, not a museum for saints. Jesus offers you healing, forgiveness, salvation, even in your brokenness. So start with Jesus and go from there."

Luke looked again at the stained-glass window to his left. He didn't usually sit this far back and had never stopped to read the script - 'in this world, you will have trouble.'

But take heart, Luke thought, *I have overcome the world.*

After the service, a few people gathered around Luke's father to thank him for the service, so he let him know he was just going to make a cup of tea.

An older man had been playing the piano in the band that night, filling in the role he had probably been rostered for originally. It took Luke a few minutes to realise why he recognised him.

"Mr Jones?" A man in his mid-fifties turned around to face Luke and his face lit up.

"Good evening Luke. I must say, that was a pretty weighty sermon this evening. If it were any heavier, we'd be Catholic!" Luke raised an eyebrow. "Because we'd have mass," he smiled. Yep, this was Chris' dad. "What can I do you for?"

"Well, I just wanted to let you know that I know Chris from school and, uh, they made it onto the footy team."

"Chris?" The older man's brow furrowed, but Luke ploughed on. If he stopped now, he didn't think he could gather the nerve to get started again.

"Yeah, they're one of my good friends at school, and it's finals this week."

"Oh, I didn't even know she'd tried out." He seemed lost, and Luke realised that it must hurt to hear something so important second hand. "She'd been wanting to for ages."

"It's kind of a big thing because the team wasn't going to allow it before but Chris is just that good." He stepped forward, determined. "I think it would mean a lot to them if you came."

Mr Jones attempted a smile, but his shoulders were slumped like a deflated balloon. "Doesn't that get confusing," he asked quietly, almost more to himself. "They, them?" Luke nodded slowly.

"Maybe, at first, but then you kind of realise that's who Chris is. To love them means to accept them, even if you don't quite get it just yet." He thought back to sitting next to his father that morning. "Just knowing that someone is there for you while you try to figure it out is enough sometimes."

"I think you're getting to be just as wise as your dad, young man." Jones tried to pass it off as a joke, but there was sincerity in his voice. "When is this game?"

"Tomorrow, down at the big footy pitch at the back of the school."

"I see," said Mr Jones, clapping Luke on the shoulder. "Thank you."

"No worries." He hoped he had made it better for Chris somehow, by stepping in.

As he turned away, Ellie approached him. She was waving a crisp $50 note.

"Hey, a bunch of people are going out for burgers and dad said we can go, as long as we go together. He said, because you're still grounded, I just have to annoy you for the rest of the night."

Luke looked up at his dad, who smiled and nodded at him.

As he headed outside with his sister, he heard someone jogging to catch up with them.

"Going for burgers?" It was Jamie.

"Yep," Ellie replied, beaming up at Jamie.

"Do you mind if I walk with you guys?"

"Not at all," Ellie said, swapping places with Luke so that she was in the middle.

"Is it okay if we have a moment to chat first?" he asked, and something in his tone told her it was not the time to protest.

"I'm just gonna hang back and wait for Caitlin, okay Luke?" she asked, placing a hand on his shoulder. She had the grace not to look too disappointed.

"Yeah, of course." His sister disappeared and the two began to walk down the hill. Eventually, Jamie broke the silence.

"I am so sorry about yesterday."

"It's okay," he mumbled. An image of Jamie from the night before rose, unbidden, to mind. His worst nightmare had come true - someone he thought was his friend, horrified by the discovery of who he truly was.

"No, it's not okay," Jamie replied ardently. "I've been thinking about it ever since yesterday. I should have said something. Man, I should have said *anything*."

"We really don't have to talk about it." Maybe he wasn't ready to have this conversation.

Suddenly, Jamie grabbed him by the arm and pulled him to the side of the footpath. "Look, I am really sorry I'm not attracted to you in the same way you feel about me, but I love you, Jamie. You're the closest thing I have to a brother, and I care about you." His voice broke towards the end of the sentence and Luke pulled him in for a hug.

"I love you too."

It wasn't the way he had always pictured it, confessing their love for each other, but maybe that was okay.

After months of trying to figure out who he was and what he wanted, and pushing his friends away in the process, maybe it was just as good to know that Jamie cared about him. That he could be friends with another guy, and they could accept him for who he was. That was at least a start.

There was a little path carved into the hill which led from the church to the beach, a mixture of short staircases and gravel footpaths which weaved behind people's houses, in between fences and crossing over little roads scattered through cul-de-sacs. As the sun set lilac and dusky rose around them, the night was filled with the scent of jasmine and backyard barbeques.

"I've been chatting to Fuddy," Jamie said eventually. The other people from church had rushed past them, including Ellie, who had stopped to give Luke a quizzical thumbs up. He nodded and smiled at her, and she had run to keep up with her friends.

"What about?"

"About you, sometimes, but also about his life and stuff. The guy I was with wasn't exactly a great conversationalist." Luke thought back to the old man staring off into space Jamie had been paired with. "He has really answered a few questions I had about faith, and life. He was also the one who encouraged me not to give up on you – he said he thought you might be working through some stuff." Luke silently thanked God for Elmer. "We had no idea what was going on for you, me and Mikayla."

"That's not how I would have told you," Luke interjected, thinking of the night before.

Jamie laughed. "Yeah, there are probably better ways." Some kids were sprawled on their bellies, scribbling pictures on the warm concrete with chalk. The boys carefully walked around them, so as not to disturb their little artworks. "I'm sorry you felt like you couldn't talk about it with us, though."

"It wasn't anything that you had done," Luke hurried to reassure him. "Just more that I realised I had a crush on my best friend's boyfriend, and I didn't think either of you would be very happy about it."

"That makes total sense," Jamie laughed. "But it doesn't mean I want to lose you as a friend." Luke bumped against his friend's arm as they walked.

"Thanks."

"Have you told your parents?"

"Yes, actually," Luke replied, "I kind of came out to them this morning."

Jamie raised an eyebrow and turned to look at his friend. "And?"

He thought back to sitting beside his dad on the bed. He had filled his mum and sister in at lunchtime, Ellie coming around the table to throw her arms around him and squealing about how awesome it was to have a gay brother. He assumed that by the end of the week, everyone in her year would have heard about it, but didn't feel too freaked out by the prospect.

"They were pretty cool about it."

"Phew," Jamie said, pretending to wipe sweat off his brow. "And how are you feeling about it all?"

"The gay thing?"

"Yeah." They passed the primary school Luke had gone to as a kid, and a surfer waxing his board on his front fence. How was he feeling about it all? Nothing had actually changed since this morning - he was still all the things he had been, with all of the same problems. He thought it over.

"Alright, I think. I mean, I'm still figuring it out, but I'll be okay."

"And the God thing?"

"You mean being a Christian?"

Jamie nodded.

"You go first," Luke replied. "How do *you* feel about it? Would you say you're a Christian?"

The other boy shrugged, staring at the ground but not really seeing it. "I never used to think about that sort of thing much, until my mum passed away. She was really into it, used to go to church every week.

At first, I didn't even believe in God, and then she kind of convinced me that he was real, but that just made me angry at him when she died. If he's that powerful, why didn't he save her, y'know?" Luke nodded. "But I haven't been as angry for a while. Talking to Fuddy really helped – he's been through some tough times as well, and really thought about how God factors into that." Luke thought about Elmer, counselling young soldiers during the war and being so close to so much pain.

"I guess I just think that, maybe there's a reason. I mean, she was in a lot of pain towards the end, and that's not how life's supposed to be. Now she's resting in peace, she's with God like she always wanted to be, and that's a good thing. Does that make sense?" He looked up at Luke, who nodded thoughtfully.

"Yeah, for sure. I mean, I haven't suffered like that, but..."

"But you know what it feels like to want God to take it away," Jamie finished.

"Yeah." They paused on the path to watch the last rays of sunset disappear, leaving a pale yellow spot on the horizon. Above them, the evening was slowly getting darker, like someone had laid a thick strip of navy paint on one side and poured water over it, spilling it into the sky.

"Do you think there's a reason for everyone's suffering?" Luke asked.

Starting his last year of high school, the one question Luke had been asked more times than he could count was "what are you going to do?" It probably referred to after school, but it felt like the anthem of his life, the immovable question mark hanging over his head. What am I going to do? And what about when it hurts?

"There's got to be." There was a conviction, a passion there Luke couldn't hear in the voice of people who had been Christians for years. "I mean, I've been through it all in my head, and I think he is real and he does matter. Watching my mum, I just came to the conclusion that there has to be something *else*. There has to be more to life than death. So God has to be important, right?"

Luke realised Jamie was right. Living didn't mean not being in pain ever again, living with God just meant it wasn't pointless. It mattered - *he* mattered.

"I think so too," Luke replied, the same conviction stirring in his voice.

"So, how are you going with God?"

"I think I'm ready to give him a proper chance. It felt for so long like I had to choose between my faith and my sexuality, but I'm starting to see that maybe I don't. Maybe I can do both."

They rounded the corner to see a bunch of their church friends crowded around some aluminium tables outside the burger joint.

Wherever he went from here, he knew his starting point was God.

15
Revelations

The next day, Luke asked his dad if he was allowed to leave the house for something school related. Once he had the all-clear, he headed down to the nursing home, feeling naked without the rest of the school group.

He headed to the reception desk to ask if he was allowed to visit Elmer Richards. The nurse made a quick call and asked Fuddy if he was up for any visitors and then called over another nurse to direct Luke. He was surprised when she led him to a small room off the side of the hall rather than the large visiting room.

"It's a dialysis day," the nurse explained in a hushed tone. "That means he'll be a little bit more quiet and maybe in a bit of pain. Be gentle with him, and if you see he's getting a bit tired, it might be time to go."

Sitting in bed, propped up by a few pillows, Fuddy was smiling as he walked in through the door. A thin plastic tube filled with blood was hooked up to a machine which beeped rhythmically, removing the waste from his body.

"You've come early this week," Fuddy said, gesturing him over. "And you're not in your school uniform. Is everything okay?" He wasn't as well dressed as he usually was, in sweatpants and an unbuttoned old polo shirt. His face was pale and his hair was mussed up at the back from lying on the pillows. Luke thought back to what he had said when they first met, about how important it was to be well dressed for entertaining guests, and felt awful. All he had thought about on the way over was his own problems.

"Maybe I'll come back another time, when you're feeling a bit better."

"Oh no, you're here now," Fuddy waved his words away impatiently. "Keep me company for a bit." Luke took a seat in the hard grey plastic chair beside him.

"I'm just taking some time off school. Well," he clarified, "some enforced time off school. I'm sorry I haven't been around on Tuesdays."

"That's okay, I understand that life gets in the way sometimes. However, you look like a man on a mission. What's on your mind today?"

Luke had practised the words he was going to say the entire walk over, but now that he was actually here, looking at his friend in this condition, he had forgotten what they were.

"I wanted to talk to you about faith." He took a deep breath. "I just feel…" He was surprised as he felt hot tears start to burn their way down his cheeks.

"A little lost?" Fuddy finished, and he nodded as they dropped off his chin and into his lap. Silently, without any fanfare, Elmer placed a box of tissues on the bed between them. "I have felt lost many times, but doubt is how you know you truly believe something. If it didn't matter, you wouldn't have to wrestle with it."

"You said you were… are attracted to men?" This topic, which had felt so taboo for so long, was now suddenly on the table, and Luke felt awkward just handling something so unfamiliar. The old man nodded, without so much as a sideways glance. "How have you kept going for so many years? You never dated? Never married? How did you handle being so... alone?"

Elmer sighed, and Luke knew that his friend understood exactly what he was asking.

"There is a great difference between being single and being alone. One comes with the territory - you don't ask the boy out, you say no when he asks you, and you trudge on, day by day. But being *alone* was never what we were created for. We were created by a God who loves perfectly and gives us family, community, friends." He gestured to the walls around him, which were covered in bookshelves. For the first time, Luke looked around him and realised he was in Fuddy's living room. Almost none of the wall was visible, covered floor to ceiling with books and photographs. Luke looked around him at the hundreds of smiling faces, all with Fuddy among them, standing for the first few shelves and, as he aged, sitting. He had been all around the world, surrounded by people of different ethnicities, ages and cultures. Some of the photos contained church buildings or houses with pictures of saints on their walls.

"Who are these people?" Luke whispered.

"They're my family," Fuddy replied. "Being adopted by God means becoming the brother of all of the other people who are part of his family, and that is an incredible privilege which has helped me not feel so alone. You have friends like that, don't you? People who love you and stick closer than brothers?"

Luke thought back to his conversation with Jamie, walking down to the beach, and nodded.

"Those people are gifts. Sometimes they will fail us, and sometimes others will be downright cruel, but in those moments, we have Jesus, who will never leave us or forsake us." The old man took Luke's hand in his own, clasping it between his rough palms. "You have to learn how to rely on them or you may be tempted some day to just give up."

All of the moments which had led up to Sunday morning came rushing back to him, overwhelming and cold as they swept over his body, but looking down at the weathered hands wrapped around his own, other memories began to mix in as well. Being accepted by his parents, the love of his sister and reconciling with Jamie. He never could have known they were coming. Sitting here surrounded by memories, he realised that the man in front of him had gone through all of that and more in his lifetime.

"I can't pretend my feelings don't matter," Luke whispered.

"Of course not!" He was surprised by the passion in Fuddy's voice. "They are a big part of what makes you who you are, but they are not *all* of who you are. You are more than your attractions or even your sins; as a Christian, you are loved by God, so much that he died for you. Your choices need to be made out of that knowledge, your identity needs to come from there.

You know, Jesus was single until he died. He never married, had sex, had a family. What he had was God and the people around him and that's all he needed. Don't narrow yourself down to that one aspect of your life."

"So where to from here?" Luke asked. He still found himself struggling to imagine the future. "I want to be a Christian, but I don't know if I can keep living this way, trying to figure it all out on my own."

"Well, once you become a Christian, there is only one path."

"Give everything up and become a monk?"

The old man chuckled. "No, that would mean hiding yourself away. Being gay doesn't mean you don't need to exist any more or God is ashamed of you. You are just as worthy of love and forgiveness as anyone else. But do you know what Jesus said when asked what the two most important things to do were?"

He thought back to the sermon from the night before. "Love the Lord your God with all your heart, soul and mind and love your neighbour as yourself."

"That's what you do from here. You love God and love others. Every morning, I wake up and I have to make the decision for myself. Sometimes it's more than every morning, it's every few hours. You just wake up and decide that you are going to follow Jesus that day. The rest follows. And some days, that might have to do with your feelings for other boys, but on others it will mean being nice to your sister, or doing the dishes for your mum, or making wise financial decisions for your company. There is so much more to you, Luke, so much more to *life* than just who you're attracted to."

He rested a hand gently on Luke's knee, the tenderness of which prompted the tears to flood back across Luke's eyes. "It won't be easy, but it will be worth it."

A few minutes later, the machine made a new sound and a nurse came in to begin unhooking Fuddy from the machine. He winced as she removed the catheter from his hand and when he reached for the button to lower the bed, his hand was trembling.

"I might hit the road, Fuddy," Luke said, placing a hand over the old man's. It was freezing cold.

"Stay," Fuddy whispered, his voice almost hoarse. "Please." His head fell back against the cushions, but his fingers gently squeezed Luke's. The young boy went outside to make a cup of tea and perused the shelves for something to read, settling on an old Agatha Christie novel. By the time he sat down again, his friend was sleeping peacefully, so he read and drank his tea as the sun began to set.

***

Time passed slowly until the big match. Luke had been surprised when his dad had asked if he wanted to go and support his friends, watching from the sidelines, but he had been over the moon. As much as he wanted to go, he wasn't planning to sneak out of the house again any time soon.

The match was on the school oval so that students from other schools or who would usually be participating in other matches could come and watch. Down on the field, Luke could see the boys preparing and Chris, with their shock of bright blue and pink hair amongst the brunettes and blondes. When they turned to scan the crowd, he shouted and waved excitedly, as did a few of their other friends from Peer Pride. Chris smiled and waved back, turning around to show them the number on their bright yellow jersey. He could tell they were scanning the crowd for someone and began to look for him too. Just as he started to lose hope, his dad called out "Martin!" and Luke turned to see Chris' father, standing at the edge of the oval, making his way over.

"Dad!" Chris called out from the field, running to meet him on the sideline. Luke watched as they embraced, father and child.

"Hey Chrissy," their dad whispered into their hair. "I'm so proud of you."

Luke's dad put an arm around him and squeezed. "I'll sit with Mr Jones, Luke, you go find your friends."

"Thanks, Dad." As he turned away to find Mikayla and Jamie, he found himself face to face with Marcus. Luke stopped himself from walking - running - away.

"Hey man," he swallowed the lump in his throat. "I'm really sorry for what I did the other day." The bruise was almost gone now, just a yellowish tinge around his left cheekbone.

He had seen Marcus at the park while walking Brick during the week, practising throwing a ball back and forth with a man who Luke assumed was his dad.

At one point, the boy had fumbled the ball and Luke could hear almost every word his father had said, standing at the edge of the park. He could never remember his dad speaking to him like that, almost anyone for that matter. But he did know how Marcus felt, as his shoulders sagged, almost as if the weight of those words were physically on his back. He knew what it felt like to be ashamed, to be frustrated at yourself, ignoring any thoughts which might be rushing to your defence because there was no point in saying them anyway. The bruise on his face was barely visible from where Luke had hit him, but perhaps, Luke realised, getting hit wasn't what hurt Marcus anymore.

Marcus swiped a hand over his face and slowly reached it out. "That's alright man. I shouldn't have said what I said." The two boys shook hands. "I don't really think you're gay," he said, scuffing his toe into the grass.

"That's not what offended me," Luke smiled as Marcus looked up, realisation coming about as slowly as an antique train. "Best of luck to you, mate, you're carrying the team now."

Mikayla was sitting on a picnic blanket in the shade, and he went over to join her.

"Can I sit with you?" he asked, squatting down. She looked up, surprised, but slowly a smile spread over her face.

"Of course." She offered him a bag of mixed lollies and he took a strawberry cloud. "I heard from Jamie that you two had a good chat on Sunday night."

"Yeah, we did. We managed to figure things out."

"I'm glad." She bit into a gummy bear and chewed as she tried to choose her words carefully. "I meant what I said the other night, Luke.

I don't care if you're gay. And I know," she held up a finger as he tried to interrupt her, and he thought, not for the first time that she would make a great teacher someday. "I know you were worried about what I would say because you had a crush on Jamie, but I never got the chance to say that I would hope to treat you the same way I would treat a girl if she had a crush on the same guy as me. With dignity, love, and a strong dose of friendly competition." Luke laughed and rolled his eyes.

"There was never any competition between us, Mickey. Jamie felt for you hard and fast."

"I know that," she said, "but I still wish I hadn't almost lost my best friend over the thought."

"I'm sorry I just ghosted you over it. I panicked."

"No kidding."

"Friends?" he asked.

"Friends," she answered, and leant over to give him a kiss on the cheek. "I don't just share my lollies with anyone."

Jamie saw his friends and started jogging over. "Are we all good now?" he asked.

"Yes, please," Luke said, grabbing another lolly and smiling at his old friend.

"Good, now tell him the plan for the formal." Jamie sat down and tore open a packet of sour straps he had brought.

"We're all going together, and we're all going to wear our special colour - I'm going to wear pink, Jamie's going to wear his signature blue and you're going to wear a black tux. Then, we're all going to get each other flowers in our signature colours - Jamie can get me a corsage, I'll get you a flower for your boutonniere and you can get Jamie one. Then, we'll all look like we match." Mikayla flashed her brilliant, evil genius smile.

"I don't know any other seventeen year old who knows the word boutonniere," Luke said, stretching out his legs in front of him. He had missed this, the ease of sitting amongst friends and figuring out the future. "But is it okay if I pick a colour too?" Both of his friends looked at him in surprise. "I just don't think black is my colour anymore."

"I'll allow it," Mikayla said, with a curt nod, "as long as you tell us which colour it is before the date so we can coordinate floral arrangements."

As they basked in the afternoon sun, watching their team and cheering them on, Luke looked between his two best friends.

Maybe they would date, and maybe it would work out and they would forget to keep him in the loop sometimes. Maybe they would break up some day and it would be awkward trying to navigate between them. But right now, his friends were trying their best and that made it worth it, no matter what happened further on down the road.

At half time, Luke ran down to the side of the pitch.

Chris had taken his position, and his number, so they were easy to spot. Tall and lanky, their only job was to keep an eye on the sides of the game. He waved to his mates as they broke the huddle and a few of them waved back, but the atmosphere was down. It was halfway and a tie, which meant anyone's game. All their hard work up to this moment felt like it had been for nought.

He yelled some encouragement to the team, and they moved their huddle to the sidelines to hear some of the ideas he had thought up for them. They all threw their hands into the centre of the circle, Luke included, and the referee blew the whistle.

The ball flew into the air.

The next half an hour, the ball switched sides half a dozen times. Chris was nervous, and fumbled it once or twice, immediately sending it over. He could remember the feeling from when he had started out - focusing on the team, rather than the game. It meant no one was watching them, though. No one expected anything out of them. He remembered that feeling too.

He ran along the white picket fence, yelling out the names of his team when they got offside and trying to direct them, cheering them on. With only a few minutes left of the game, the ball centimetres from the end, the sixth touch.

Changeover.

Marcus' ball.

Not enough time to get it from one side of the field to the other.

More than his fair share of the other team crowding around to shadow him, the strongest player on the field and try to figure out what he was thinking.

He looks up and sees what Marcus sees - the only free player, alone on the outskirts.

He bomb kicks the ball, sending it spinning across the green.

The last will be first, thinks Luke, as Chris catches it.

The nose hits the grass.

The crowd goes wild.

The team merged into one giant scrum of black and yellow, cheering and screaming as they pushed into each other, clapping Chris on the back and waving their shirts in the air. A few boys try to lift Chris, no one with enough clear sense to figure it out. Luke jumps the fence and joins three other boys in making a human chair, hoisting Chris onto their shoulders.

They plunged into the tidal wave of joy.

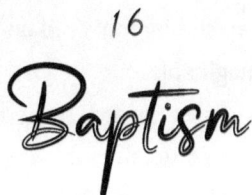

16

Baptism

That Tuesday was the last trip to the nursing home for the term, and Luke walked to the school gates in a t-shirt and jeans, waiting to join his friends.

As they crowded into the visitor's centre, he was struck again by how empty it was and decided that, even though he had met his volunteering hours for the program, he would still pop in and see Fuddy when he had some spare time.

His elderly friend had reprised his usual seat by the window and was reading a weather worn novel. Today he was wearing a vermillion neck tie which matched his pocket square and complemented the flecks of orange in the tartan of his sports coat. He looked like he was ready to sit for a portrait, his hair slicked to the side and his moustache combed just so.

"Luke!" he called out, waving him over.

"Hey, Fuddy," he smiled, walking over.

"Interested in a game of chess?" The board was already set up in front of him, the pieces all in orderly rows.

"Yes, but first, I have a favour to ask you." Luke told him his plan for the formal, and the old man smiled widely.

"That is definitely something I would be able to help you out with."

The two made their way down the corridor and back to Fuddy's room, where he walked over to two sliding mirrored doors and pulled them apart. Inside was every colour imaginable.

Bowties, neckties and pocket squares in perfect gradient from red, to orange, to yellow, to green, to blue, to violet.

"Take your pick," the old man grinned, waving a shaky hand up and down the rows. "I have a few suits too, although I don't know if I was as tall as you, even in my prime. I don't get barely enough use out of them these days." Hung in the closet were a dozen suits, waiting like dancers for their partners. There were a few shades of sombre black and grey, pin-stripes reminiscent of days in the office, but what caught Luke's eye was a neat navy blue suit. He had seen it in one of the photographs of Fuddy, sitting on a dirt floor somewhere dark, surrounded by what must have been about a hundred children of all ages, grinning and trying to squeeze their faces into the frame. He stood out amongst them, his pale skin and wavy corn-coloured hair. Luke pulled it out and held the hanger to his shoulders.

"Should be just long enough," the old man said, stepping back into a corner to admire the fit. "Must have been meant to be." He went to the closet and ran his hand down the ties. "This one," he said, pulling out a dusty lavender and placing it in Luke's hands with his own. "It will perfectly match your hair now and when it grows back."

"I'll get them back to you straight after the formal."

"No, no, you keep it." The old man grinned, and Luke could see a glimmer of the young man he used to be, cheeky, and confident, and kind. "What am I going to do with it once I'm gone?" He winked and closed

Luke's fingers around the tie and the two walked back outside, Luke hanging up his suit on the windowsill to keep it off the floor. They sat opposite each other around the table.

"Alright, now I'm ready for a rematch."

They sat across from each other, playing chess until the sun started to go down and the nurses began to usher out the few guests who were still lingering with their loved ones.

Fuddy opened the board, placing forward a white pawn.

Luke responded in turn with his own pawn.

They repeated their actions, a white knight taking one of Luke's lonely pieces.

"Ready to admit defeat?"

"Not just yet."

He brought forward his own knight, a black horse riding to defend its king. His king wriggled this way and that.

"Thank you for still wanting to talk to me, even after I sort of gave up on coming for a bit there."

"That really is no trouble to me, Luke," Fuddy smiled as he figured out his next move. The white knight advanced, inching closer and closer, almost threatening to take out his queen. He slid her to the left, out of harm's way.

"Borrowing a suit isn't the only favour I wanted to ask you."

The white knight took a pawn, now in prime position to take either his queen or rook.

"I've got a special event to invite you to at the end of the week." In a bold move, Luke flung his bishop far over to the right.

"Whatever it is, I would love to come," Fuddy replied, his confusion turning to joy as he realised what Luke had done.

"That looks like checkmate, by the way," Luke smiled. Whether his pieces moved to the left or the right, his king was now trapped by the queen and bishop.

"It looks like I've taught you well," Fuddy said, shaking his hand. Luke didn't want to admit he had

been up late at night, watching and practising manoeuvres he had learned on YouTube. However, despite it all, Fuddy had taught him far more than chess over the term.

So he simply replied, "Thanks."

Luke walked from the nursing home to school to wait for his friends, reversing the trip he had made so often with them. As the two walked out, they dropped each other's hands. Luke almost blurted out that it was alright, but paused, took a deep breath and smiled. They were trying not to exclude him, at least when the three of them were together, and that meant a lot.

"I think I'll be wearing navy," Luke said, swinging the suit off his shoulder. Safely encased in a drycleaning bag, he unzipped it slightly to show his friends.

"Wow, that's awesome!" Jamie grinned in approval. "Where did you get that?"

"An old friend gave it to me," he replied.

"Luke, I'm not meant to see your suit until the big day!" Mikayla rolled her eyes.

"We're not getting married, Mickey. Besides, I thought it would help you figure out the colour scheme for the evening."

"It will, I suppose," she acquiesced, "and don't call me Mickey."

The three began the ascend back up the big hill in the direction of his house, Luke in the centre of his two friends.

"I figured out who I'm going to write about, by the way," he said to Jamie. "For the modern history thing?"

"Oh yeah?"

"Bayard Rustin was a gay African American man who helped Reverend Martin Luther King during the civil rights movement," Luke began. "Due to his sexuality, he was always in the background. He didn't want to shift the focus of what he thought was so important onto himself by taking the lead, and in the end was arrested on trumped up charges. However, he taught Martin Luther King about non-violent protest and helped organise the Freedom Rides. He was a Quaker, a Christian man, who ended up campaigning for gay rights until his death in 1987."

"I've never heard of him," Mikayla said, listening in.

"The church at the time wasn't ready to accept him. He was living with a man he probably would have married if it was legal and got convicted of crimes he was only exonerated for after he died. They rejected him, but he still did his best to help where he could."

"Are you sure this is who you want to write about? I'll be honest with you; I don't know how your presentation is going to go at school."

Luke nodded. "I think I'm okay with that. He was misunderstood by the people of his era and wasn't acknowledged for all the good he did. I think he fits the task well - an everyday person doing the best with what they have."

His friend nodded. "Is that what you want to do? Try and change the world?"

"I'm at least ready to try," Luke said, thinking back to Fuddy and the life he had lived.

"And how does your faith factor into all of that?" Mikayla said, as they reached the steps of the old brick church.

"I think I'm beginning to figure it out." He sat on the steps, his friends sandwiching him between them. "My faith is a part of who I am. It's important to me, I think it has been for a long time - not just something my parents believe, or something I've grown up with, but actually close to my heart. I don't think being gay has to hold me back from that. Actually, I think it's also a part of what makes me who I am. By being single, I can be freed up to help out around church more, get involved in ministries I wouldn't be able to with a partner or a family. I can understand other people who are single, even if they haven't chosen to be, like my parents get along well with married couples and other parents.

"So, we won't be trying to find you a cute guy?" Although he knew she was cracking a joke, Luke sighed.

"No, I don't think so, at least not any time soon. I'm okay with being single at the moment. I think a lot of what's been going on for me the past few weeks was the thought of losing you guys and being alone. I realised that maybe it doesn't have to be that way."

"Not while we're around," Jamie said, bumping against his arm. "Sorry mate, you're not getting rid of us any time soon."

"Good, because I'm definitely going to need you guys." He hooked an arm through the crook of their elbows. "I don't know what the future holds, but something my dad said the other night really stuck with me - I'm going to start with Jesus and go from there."

***

Standing waist deep in the pool on the top of the hill, he smiled at his friends, gathered on the rocks.

Mikayla was talking to Chris, looking a little out of her depth but at least she was trying.

Jamie was standing there with his Dad, trying to use him as a human shield from Ellie.

Elmer Richards was sitting in a wheelchair further back, a nurse accompanying him while Luke's mum introduced herself.

And his dad was standing next to him, wearing nothing but a pair of board shorts and a wide grin.

"Thank you for gathering here with me today," he began, his hand on his son's shoulder. "Today we are celebrating Luke's decision to accept Jesus for himself. Baptism is a public declaration of something which has happened in the heart - it symbolises the washing away of sin, dying to oneself and rising again as Christ was risen. As one proud father once said, 'For this my son was dead and is alive again; he was lost and is found'." He turned to his son. "I am so proud of you, Luke."

"Speech!" Chris called out from the crowd, but before he could say anything, it started to sprinkle. Everyone gasped as the mist settled on them, cool after the heat of the day. The sun shone through the rain, and above them formed a rainbow.

Luke grinned up at his dad. "I don't have much to say other than, I'm ready."

His dad squeezed his arm and placed a hand between Luke's shoulder blades.

He blocked his nose as his father lowered him into the water.

For a second, there was silence and all he could see was the light of the sun above him.

His dad pulled him back up.

And they began to celebrate.

Author's note

If you're reading this, then I assume you've read my book. Thank you for getting through it. A lot of late nights (and free periods) went into trying to produce something worth reading.

I am not gay, and I will never truly understand the struggles of what that must be like as a teenager trying to wrestle with your sexuality or gender, especially as a kid growing up in a Christian household. However, I have a few friends who are part of the LGBTQI+ community and this book is dedicated to them.

As a high school English teacher, I understand the importance of seeing yourself reflected in what you read and watch - there is a lot of great secular fiction out there written for, by and about the LGBTQ+ community, but while there are some theological books, I noticed there isn't really any fiction, anything a teenager would (hopefully) be interested in. I wanted to write something for those kids, and their parents, friends, churches and people who love them.

I hope I have done that.

I want to acknowledge that there is a growing movement in today's church of gay Christians getting married and still being active members. My father-in-law asked me why I didn't give Luke someone who was attracted to him too, and I'm sure there will be people who are disappointed that he decided to stay single. In short, that would have been an entirely other novel.

I do not want to invalidate the story of Christians who do pursue relationships, but to try and do the theological footwork of what that means for Christians, and in particular young gay Christians, was not the purpose of this novel. However, if that's something you're curious about, I want to encourage you to find someone you trust to talk to about all of the complicated ins and outs of being a gay Christian.

I just wanted to explore whether someone can even be attracted to the same sex and be saved (the answer, I hope is clear, is yes) and how the church can interact with those Christians (the answer, I hope is clear, is better). I wanted a character with gay and queer friends, and Christians who love and accept him. I wanted him to have awkward conversations with people that ended well, and to know that he is loved by God first and foremost.

If you are interested in exploring the actual workings of Christianity and the LGBTQI+ community, I would highly recommend these books by gay Christians:

> The Plausibility Problem, Ed Shaw
> Is God Anti-Gay?, Sam Allberry

The moment when Luke sits on the kitchen floor is actually based off something I read in Ed Shaw's book, where he talks about his own kitchen floor moments, heartbroken and overwhelmed with loneliness or doubts. It is such a vivid image which has stuck with me ever since.

Similarly, by including a character like Chris in this story, who is wrestling with their gender, I wasn't aiming to theologically affirm or deny the trans and non-binary community, including those who are Christian. I wanted to acknowledge those people, and explore how the church can interact with them (the answer, I hope is clear, is better).

If you are interested in exploring the topic further, a great book by another gay Christian is:

Talking Points: Transgender, Vaughn Roberts

This book is dedicated to my friend B.B., who inspires me to be a better Christian every time I see him. I pray that some day he would feel able to be himself with his family, but until then, I want to be the best sort of adopted family I can.

This book also goes out to my two gay friends with the initial K, who haven't felt welcome in a church since they decided to embrace their sexuality freely and openly - I pray that one day, we would be the sort of church that is a hospital for the sick and not just a hotel for those who are pretending to be healthy.

I would like to thank Barbara, for being the first to set eyes on a skeleton of a draft and help me turn it into a living, breathing story. You are my Fuddy, and have been just as much help in learning how to play life's games. Tom, for finally getting around to reading this and supporting me in my dream of getting it published. The Croswellers, whose ministry, house and love for each other I have shamelessly plagiarised. Jiarn, for teaching me about football and being my novel-writing cheerleader.

I want to especially thank my mum, who always told me I could write well, and my dad for being the closest he could ever get to my heavenly father.

This book also goes out to anyone who is trying to figure themselves out.

Start with Jesus and go from there.

If you, or someone you know, is struggling with their mental health, please reach out.

Kids Helpline: 1800 55 1800
Lifeline: 13 11 14
QLife (for LGBTQIA+ specific support): 1800 184 527 (3pm–midnight AEST)

Colours

www.ingramcontent.com/pod-product-compliance
Lightning Source LLC
Chambersburg PA
CBHW051920240626
47153CB00004B/1301